First published in Great Britain in 2024 by Farshore
An imprint of HarperCollins*Publishers*
1 London Bridge Street, London SE1 9GF

farshore.co.uk

HarperCollins*Publishers*
Macken House, 39/40 Mayor Street Upper, Dublin 1, D01 C9W8

Text copyright © Nicky Smith-Dale 2024
Illustration copyright © Sarah Horne 2024

The moral rights of the author and illustrator have been asserted

ISBN 978 0 00 860034 1

Printed and bound in the UK using 100% renewable electricity at
CPI Group (UK) Ltd

1

A CIP catalogue record for this title is available from the British Library.

NICKY SMITH-DALE

ILLUSTRATED BY
Sarah HORNE

BETTY STEADY

AND THE TOAD WITCH

for Miles and Cassie

CRAG OF INSTABILITY

Mount CRUMBLE DOWN

WOBBLY ROCK

NOT TODAY, THANK YOU!

Noxious VALLEY of THE SNAILS

N

N.N.N.N. N.N.N.N. EAST

W ——— E

S.S.S.S. S.S.S.S. WEST

S

MAP of WOBBLY ROCK

HULLO!

BLEE BLAH BLAH...

 ong ago and far away – between the invention of the laundry basket and the first panda in space – there lived a girl. Actually, there lived lots of girls, but I'm not going to tell you about them all because we'd be here forever, and I've got to make my bed before my mum gets home. (Authors have chores too, you know.)

I'm going to tell you about a *particular* girl. A special girl, called Betty Steady.

At twelve years old, she was expert in swordplay and combat. Daughter of two great knights – long since passed – she stood tall and dazzling, blessed with unmatched strength, speed and stylish hair. Faster than an angry goose, more powerful than an ogre in yoga pants, she protected the people of Wobbly Rock fearlessly.

Ruled over by King Nutmeg, Wobbly Rock rested high on the side of Mount Crumbledown. Over the years, the usual rotters – like the three-eyed dribble dragons, the legion of battle-pigs, and the terrifying army of the Toad Witch – had attempted to storm the castle walls. But they'd always been trounced by Betty Steady, the Guardian of Wobbly Rock.

'SHE SOUNDS UTTERLY BRILL!'

I hear you say. Well, you're right. She *was* utterly brill. But the thing about being utterly brill is that sometimes you get a bit too big for your boots. And you might just find that someone wants to cut you down to size . . .

A quick note about me

efore we continue with the story, I must introduce myself properly. I am respected author, Salvador Catflap. There aren't many writers in Wobbly Rock (in fact, it's just me and a farmer called Clammy Pete, who makes up poems about bees) but storytelling is a noble tradition that I take very seriously. And it's just as well, because apparently, some people in your world don't

believe Wobbly Rock exists. The cheek! Our lands might be wild and remote but Wobbly Rock is as real as pork pie. It lies within the nostrils of time and space itself, where historical accuracy turns upside down and does somersaults.

Contained within these pages is the full and glorious history of this great land and its remarkable heroine. Unless of course my pen starts to run out, in which case I might just write the silly bits.

'Where is she?' King Nutmeg drummed his fingers along the arm of his throne and blew a wet raspberry. He was a long man, whose face looked like someone who'd yawned and got stuck.

'Told you I should have gone with her,' said Figg.

'Can't we start the feast anyway?' complained

King Nutmeg. 'My tummy's growling like a bad-tempered badger.'

'Best to wait, Your Majesty.' Figg – who was an imp no taller than a large carrot, with wonky antlers – studied the crowd of courtiers staring anxiously at the castle door. 'This rabble might get worried.'

'**WORRIED?**'

the king roared.

'Who'd doubt the Guardian of Wobbly Rock? Figg, you do talk turnip sometimes.'

'Oh, come on,' said Figg. 'Betty always goes charging in without thinking. She doesn't even stop to look at my BUM.'

'Excuse me?' said the king.

'My *Biweekly Unabridged Memo* of the most pressing matters in the kingdom, Your Majesty.' Figg scratched his beard, which lay patchy over his green skin. 'Betty doesn't like to trouble her brain when her biceps can do the thinking.'

'Oh, nonsense and nappies, Figg. She knows what she's doing.' The king tried to wave the thought away, but his adviser's words had indeed sent a surge of unease through his chest. Perhaps riding out unaccompanied to vanquish a GIANT THREE-HEADED VIPER was a stretch too far, even for Betty.

He glanced over at his twin daughters, Pam and Pamm, who were nibbling on each other's fingernails. He had to admit – they did seem a *little* concerned about the welfare of their dear friend.

7

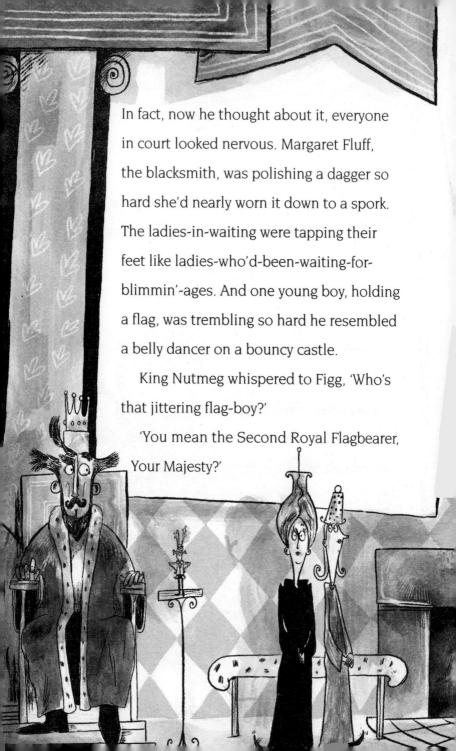

In fact, now he thought about it, everyone
in court looked nervous. Margaret Fluff,
the blacksmith, was polishing a dagger so
hard she'd nearly worn it down to a spork.
The ladies-in-waiting were tapping their
feet like ladies-who'd-been-waiting-for-
blimmin'-ages. And one young boy, holding
a flag, was trembling so hard he resembled
a belly dancer on a bouncy castle.

King Nutmeg whispered to Figg, 'Who's
that jittering flag-boy?'

'You mean the Second Royal Flagbearer,
Your Majesty?'

'If you say so,' said the king.

Figg took a deep breath. 'He's Johnny Logflume, son of the First Royal Flagbearer, Donnie Logflume. And brother of the Third Royal Flagbearer, Ronnie Log–'

'All right, Figg,' said the king. 'Just tell him to stop shaking. He's making me tense.'

But before the imp had a chance to move, a distinctive sound clattered through the castle wall. The *clip-clop-squelch* of approaching hooves.

King Nutmeg let out a laugh like thunder. 'There! Hear that, Figg? Told you she was coming back, you big dolly-doubter!'

When the First Royal Guard pulled open the doors, a stunning white stallion was standing in the mud. It was Betty's faithful horse, Simon Anderson. Gorgeous Simon Anderson, with his glittering mane, his eyes of sapphire, his tiger-print cycling shorts. The courtiers gasped. Not because Simon Anderson was SO DREAMY – although he was – but because there was a cloaked figure slumped on his saddle, like a rag doll whose stuffing had been pulled out by a crazed toddler.

'Heaven's handkerchiefs!' cried Lady Mayfly, the most illustrious elder at court. 'Is that Betty?'

'Jolly hard to tell,' replied retired knight and all-round nice guy, Sir Loin of Beef.

As the mystery figure let out a muffled groan, the king stood up. 'First Royal Guard, what are you waiting for?' he cried.

10

The First Royal Guard
wanted to tell the king that he
was waiting for his birthday, because
he was hoping to get a new train set. But he
quickly realised that wasn't what the king meant
at all, and hurried to lead Simon Anderson
inside. After he helped the figure down, and
pulled back the cloak, the room went silent.
Indeed, it *was* Betty Steady, but she looked

PROPER ROUGH.

'That blasted viper got me,' Betty murmured, her face pale and smeared with mud. Hunched like a wilted spinach leaf, she steadied her tall frame on Simon Anderson's reins. Blood dripped down her chin and her wet brown curls clung to her cheeks like a gang of tired slugs.

'Betty?' cried the king. 'Are you hurt?'

Betty approached the throne, grimacing with each slow step. 'Forgive me, Your Majesty.' She held out a shaking hand to the princesses. 'Oh, Pam and Pamm, I have failed you, my friends.' As she passed the Second Royal Flagbearer, she stumbled. 'Johnny Logflume?' She looked up and clutched his tunic. **'I HAVE DISGRACED YOUR FLAG, JOHNNY LOGFLUME!'**

Johnny Logflume looked around awkwardly. 'Is she all right?'

Betty slid to the floor. **'THE VENOM IS TAKING HOLD!**

I CAN SEE SPOTS! I CAN SEE INTO NEXT PANCAKE DAY!'

'My goodness!' cried Figg, rushing to her side. 'Where did it bite you?'

'Figg?' whispered Betty. Her voice wobbled like an uneven cafe table. 'Is that you? Come closer, dear imp.'

The imp clutched her hand. 'Don't give up, Betty. You can fight this.'

'There's something I've always wanted to ask you . . .' Betty leaned her head against Figg's. 'Something important.'

'Of course, Great Guardian. Ask me anything.' Figg's scrawny chest rattled wildly. 'Anything!'

As the crowd listened in flabbergasted disbelief, Betty let out a weak cough and looked the imp in the eyes. 'Would you . . .' Her words were punctuated with shallow gasps. 'Would you please . . . please take my sword?' She pulled the great weapon from her scabbard.

'Oh, Betty.' Figg's eyes brimmed with tears.

'It would be my honour.'

'Take it, little imp. Take it away.' Betty cracked a smile. 'Clean off the snake slime, then give it a polish for me, will you? While **I PARTY MY FACE OFF.'**

The imp screwed up his forehead. 'Huh?'

Betty leaped to her feet, did three cartwheels, and grabbed Johnny Logflume's flag. **'NO ONE CAN DEFEAT THE GUARDIAN OF WOBBLY ROCK!'** She waved the custard-yellow flag high in the air and wiggled her hips. 'That viper didn't stand a chance.'

The king beamed. 'Well, tickle my belly with a fluffy duster – she did it!'

As Pam jumped on Pamm's back and started a chant of 'BOOGLE-OOGLE-BLIM-BLAM!' Betty ran seven laps around the room, giving out a series of high fives. But Figg, the only sour face in a tidal wave of smiles, huffed to himself and marched away to his office to work on his BUM.

14

Chapter 2

 fter a traditional feast of roast grouse, fermented cabbage and those fruit-corner yoghurts, King Nutmeg lifted his tankard of ale.

'Raise your glasses to the Guardian of Wobbly Rock!' he said.

'THE GUARDIAN OF WOBBLY ROCK!' repeated the courtiers – all except Lady Mayfly, who, after one too many cherryades, misheard him and shouted, 'THE CARDIGAN OF KNOBBLY SOCKS!'

Now that Betty had cleaned her muddy face and detangled her curly hair, she felt like her usual self – elegant and statuesque and ready for everyone to tell her how fabulous she was. Dressed in an embellished red tunic, with a dagger tucked into her waistband, she stood as tall as a full-grown knight. Rumour had it, her great-great-grandmother had been half giant and one-eighth ice-cream van.

Betty was given the seat of honour alongside her faithful steed Simon Anderson. Her handsome stallion sat upright in his chair with his tiger-print cycling shorts on full display. Now, you might think a horse sitting upright would look a bit awkward, but I'll have you know,

Simon Anderson looked mega classy because he was just so darn DISHY. You should have seen how stunning he was, tucking into his second helping of fermented cabbage. Swoon!

'I'd jolly love to hear how you nobbled that viper, Betty!' said Sir Loin of Beef.

Betty gave a powerful laugh and slapped the retired knight on the shoulder, nearly knocking him head first into Pamm. 'Oh, it was easy. When that stupid snake tried to bite me, I sliced his first head clean off. **BINGO!** Then I chopped off his second, quick as the first. **YANKEE DOODLE!** Finally, with a backflip, I cut off the third. **POLLY PUT THE KETTLE ON!'**

Figg, who'd joined the feast late and still had a face like a soggy sandwich, rolled his eyes.

'Good golly, you *are* amazing,' said Pam. Although the twin princesses were both petite and copper-haired, you could always tell them apart by their headwear. While Pam sported a crown of

freshly cut flowers, Pamm preferred a crown of
freshly cut bread.

'I can't believe we get to be best friends with
such a VIP,' said Pamm, adjusting
her doughy headpiece. 'Hey,
do you want to
come to ours for a
sleepover tonight?
We can play *pin the wig
on the weasel* again.'
'Love to,' said Betty.
'You know that's my
absolute favourite game.
I'll be there, with sprinkles on.
Unless, of course, something urgent
and terrifying happens. Then I'd have to ride out
and save the day as usual. But that's not likely
anytime soon, is it? Haha!'

'Hahaha!' said Pam. 'No way.'

'HAHAHAHA!' said Pamm. 'As if.'

Just then, one of the night guards burst through the door. 'Something urgent and terrifying has happened!' he shouted.

'Trembling teaspoons!' cried the king. 'What is it?'

'Your Majesty,' stammered the guard. 'An ogre's been spotted wandering the forest.'

Betty gasped and leaped from her seat. 'An ogre?'

'Nasty beasts,' said Sir Loin of Beef. 'We can't jolly risk it coming too close.'

'Then it must be stopped,' said the king. 'A team of our best fighters will send that petulant monster packing.'

'No, Your Majesty.' Betty clutched her chest and flared her nostrils proudly. 'I will go alone.'

'Blow me down with a beach ball!' cried the king. 'It's far too dangerous.'

Betty looked around the room, at the troubled faces and empty yoghurt pots. The weight of responsibility was heavy, but protecting this incredible kingdom was her one job (except of

course for her second job of glue-stick monitor, but that didn't tend to lead to quite so much sword fighting). 'Trust me, oh wise king,' she said. 'I will single-handedly defeat this foul creature. And I will ride at first light.'

At dawn, Betty was still fast asleep. When she finally woke up, a little after nine, she spent a good twenty minutes removing a piece of sweetcorn from her teeth, before she remembered her mission. In a fluster, she got dressed before swinging by Margaret Fluff's forge, where the smell of burning metal and breakfast burritos filled the air.

'Is my axe ready?' asked Betty.

'Aye,' said the blacksmith, putting down her breakfast burrito and handing over the sharpened axe. 'But – oh, Great Guardian – I beg you to wear your armour this time. Ogres are known to carry serious weapons. Hammers. Daggers. Grapefruit

spoons. Believe me, you don't want one of those stuck in your backside.'

Betty frowned. 'Oh, twaddle cakes!' she said. Didn't the blacksmith realise she could outfight anyone? 'I'm the Guardian of Wobbly Rock. I don't need heavy armour.'

Margaret Fluff scratched her sooty nose. 'Some chainmail at least?'

Betty sighed and put her hands on her hips.

'Listen up, Sally Sunshine. **I DON'T NEED NO STINKING ARMOUR!'**

'All right, all right,' said the blacksmith as she went back to her spicy breakfast. 'Just be careful.'

'YOU be careful,' muttered Betty, marching away.

Five minutes later, as she was saddling up Simon Anderson by the great castle gates, Lady Mayfly and Sir Loin of Beef slunk up next to her like two eager penguins.

'I'm sure you're going to show that ogre who's boss, my dear,' said Lady Mayfly. 'But I just want to check . . . You do remember the three golden rules of bamboozling a beast?'

Betty exhaled. She didn't have time for this.

'Rule one,' said Lady Mayfly. 'Approach from high ground for the best viewpoint. Rule two. Stay upwind, so the beast can't smell you. Rule three. Have fun!'

'Yes, yes, yes,' said Betty, throwing a hooded blue cape over her best fighting clothes.

'Are you quite sure you don't jolly want me to accompany you?' asked Sir Loin of Beef.

Betty'd had enough of all this rubbish. Why didn't anyone believe in her? 'I'll be fine!' she snapped.

'But I could help –'

Betty huffed and put her hands on her hips. 'Listen up, Sally Sunshine. I DON'T NEED NO STINKING HELP! From either of you.'

Lady Mayfly and Sir Loin of Beef took a step back
in unison and chorused, 'Well, SO-RREEEE . . .'

But Betty didn't care if they were offended. She
had to get her bum on this horse and her head in
the game. Climbing on to Simon Anderson, she
looked out across the horizon, down the steep
slope of Mount Crumbledown, beyond the Noxious
Valley of the Snails, and up to the Forest of Dust.
That grotty ogre was out there somewhere, and she
was going to find it.

'Guardian?' Figg's voice squeaked behind her. 'One thing before you go.'

'Oh, come on.' Betty turned around. 'Not you too.'

The imp scurried up with a handful of papers. 'You've forgotten to sign the risk assessment.'

'You've got to be kidding,' Betty said. She put her feet in the stirrups and grabbed the reins.

'And,' Figg said breathlessly, 'there's an updated Beast and Fiend Policy in my most recent BUM. I've got you another copy here, in case you misplaced the first.'

Betty groaned. 'Listen up, Sally Sunshine'. **I DON'T NEED NO STINKING PAPERWORK!**'

Figg raised one of his green eyebrows. 'Well, you're not going anywhere without signing this form,' he said. 'It's protocol.'

'Protocol?' scoffed Betty. 'Of course! I'll be sure to tell the ogre, "Oh, *I'm sorry, we can't fight. Some jobsworth imp says we have to read fifty pages of brain-vomit first.*" Come on, Simon Anderson, let's get outta here.'

Figg scrunched up his face like a used tissue. He wasn't going to let Betty's arrogance get in the way of proper health and safety regulations. And if the only way to ensure the rules were followed was to supervise this mission himself, then so be it.

Unseen – and with the paperwork shoved into his waistcoat – Figg clambered up Simon Anderson's back leg and clung on to his tiger-print cycling shorts.

Completely unaware of the imp, Betty took a deep breath. 'RIDE SWIFTLY, NOBLE SIMON ANDERSON . . .' She held her sword skywards as Simon Anderson gave an extremely noble snort.

'LET'S GO LICK THE TOENAILS OF ADVENTURE!'

Chapter
3

 ave you ever instantly regretted a decision? Done something so daft that you wondered if your brain had temporarily turned to donkey dung?

Well, that's how Figg felt as he clung to the backside of a charging horse, getting battered and biffed like a swingball in a storm. Not to mention the gassy emissions squeaking through the stallion's cycling shorts. Simon Anderson had definitely eaten his fair share of fermented cabbage the night before.

Betty, however, was oblivious to the imp's presence, and rode on with fire in her heart, grit in her belly and the hokey-cokey stuck in her head. Avoiding the Noxious Valley of the Snails, she guided speedy Simon Anderson over meandering paths and approached the Forest of Dust from the lowest ground to the west. As they finally crossed into the thick woodland, Betty pulled Simon Anderson to a stop next to a babbling stream.

. By now – dear reader – I'm guessing you're wondering what the Forest of Dust looked like. Well, simply close your eyes and picture a place we all know and love – the **TOXIC FOREST OF ETERNAL FIRE.** Except, instead of the blazing, poisonous inferno part, think of a calm woodland with a lovely splattering of pink pixie dust. (And if you don't know what the **TOXIC FOREST OF ETERNAL FIRE** looks like, then you've never lived! You really should go sometime. It's lovely in the spring.)

Anyway, after tying Simon Anderson to a tree, Betty took a long drink from the stream and cried, 'Oooooh-eeeee, I love the great outdoors.'

Figg was dizzier than a Twix in a tumble drier, but he still had an eye for health and safety. Clambering off Simon Anderson, he glared at Betty. 'I do hope that's sanitary drinking water,' he panted.

Betty's mouth dropped. 'Figg?!' she cried. 'What in the name of digestive biscuits are you doing here?'

The imp coughed smugly. 'Well, if you can't follow simple procedures, I'm afraid you need a chaperone.'

Betty's face turned a shade of rhubarb jam. 'You sneaky stowaway! You filthy fibber!' she roared. If she couldn't be trusted to vanquish an ogre on her own, the world had gone completely bananas!

'And worry not,' said Figg, unfolding a sheet of paper. 'I've brought the risk assessment. Now, let's see. Point number one. Watch out for traps underfoot –'

'You can chuck the risk assessment down the privy for all I care!' Betty threw herself on the mud, which shimmered with pixie dust. As Simon Anderson sighed with impatience, she looked up at the sky. **'OH, HEAVENLY HANDS OF FATE, WHY, OF ALL PEOPLE, DID YOU HAVE TO SEND THE SNIVELLING IMP!'**

Figg crossed his arms. 'If you'd followed my

instructions, I wouldn't have come at all.'

'Well, I'm stuck with you now,' grumbled Betty. 'I can't leave you alone in the woods – you've got all the strength and courage of a dishcloth.'

'And you've got the IQ of a toilet brush!' said Figg. 'I assure you, I'll be more help than hindrance.'

'*Help*? Don't talk turnip!' Betty rubbed her temples. Everything would be so much simpler without other people. Or imps.

'Believe me, I know more about survival than you do,' said Figg, gazing up at the trees looming ahead. 'Hmmm . . . We're on lower ground than we should be.' He licked his finger and put it in the air. 'And there's a north-north-north-north-north-north-north-north-north-easterly wind. Which means we're downwind from the ogre. He might smell us coming.'

'Twaddle cakes with raspberries on!' said Betty. 'My smell won't give me away. I've got armpits like

a fresh meadow.' She took a big sniff to prove her point, which unfortunately timed perfectly with one of Simon Anderson's silent, deadly (yet incredibly elegant) cabbage toots.

Figg pinched his nose. 'I'm afraid the *second* of the three golden rules of bamboozling a beast state that we must stay upwind –'

'Rules are for fools, baby.'

'While the *first* suggests we should approach from high ground –'

'RULES ARE FOR FOOLS!'

Betty grabbed Figg's face and squeezed his lips shut. 'If you're coming with me, you can keep *schtum.*'

Eventually, after a lot of grumbling from all sides, Betty, Figg and Simon Anderson continued into the Forest of Dust. Although Figg was relieved to have a more comfortable seat (clinging to the back of Betty's tunic), he still wore a big, sulky frown.

When they were deep into the glittering woodland, Betty finally noticed a set of ogre prints in the mud. 'Aha!' she said, guiding Simon Anderson up a steep slope.

'Be careful,' whispered Figg. 'We've got no cover here.'

'Is Nappy-Bum Baby scared?' Betty pinched Figg's green cheek and gave it a wobble. 'Don't worry. I'll protect you.'

34

'I am NOT a Nappy-Bum Baby,' Figg said through gritted teeth.

Betty laughed. 'I think baby needs his sleep.'

'Don't patronise me!' snapped the imp. 'I have a first-class degree in Castle Administration, I speak five languages and I can recite the eighty-seven times table standing on my head.'

With a *whoosh*, something metal hurtled towards them from the top of the slope and landed behind Betty.

A deep voice bellowed, 'I CAN WHIFF HUMAN! AND PONGY LITTLE IMP!'

'Get down!' Betty cried.

Figg cowered behind Betty on Simon Anderson's back as an enormous ogre lumbered down the hill towards them. It was as tall as a double-decker bus and as wide as a downstairs loo, with skin like a snooker table. It stomped over the forest floor, spitting through rotting teeth, 'I'LL BIFF YOU UP PROPER!' With a snort, it raised its mighty

hand, which actually looked more like five jumbo sausages glued to a frisbee.

Swallowing down a big sandwich of fear, Betty took out her sword, kicked Simon Anderson into action (causing another untimely blast of fermented cabbage gas) and rode towards the ogre. But, as she came close enough to see the ogre's bulging muscles and crusty nose, she felt something she'd never felt before. A sudden panic that this big, beefy bozo might just get the better of her.

'Pull yourself together, Betty!' she muttered to herself. 'The people of Wobbly Rock are counting on you.'

As Figg clung on nervously, Betty took a deep breath and did what she always did before a great battle. She closed her eyes and summoned the strength of the trees, the power of the wind and the confidence of a really cool person in leather trousers.

With her sword held high, Betty charged at the ogre. Simon Anderson raced at top speed, his

mane blowing majestically in the wind, his cycling shorts giving him maximum flexibility. As they came towards the ogre, Betty swung her weapon and landed a blow. The beast flinched and toppled backwards on to the grass.

'HICKORY DICKORY DOCK!' Betty cried, like a really cool person in leather trousers.

But the creature got straight back on to its feet, brandishing an unusual-looking blade.

Peeping out from behind Betty, Figg shrieked, 'It's got a grapefruit spoon!'

Quicker than you can say *tutti frutti*, the ogre threw the spoon towards Betty. OOF! It struck her on the backside. Betty yelped and fell backwards off her horse, tumbling to the muddy ground. As Simon Anderson reared up in panic, Betty plucked the spoon from her bottom. It throbbed like a thousand angry bee stings.

Still perched on Simon Anderson, Figg didn't have a chance to remind Betty that she should have worn armour, because the ogre was coming towards them like a big bowling ball of rage. Hastily, Betty grabbed her axe and flung it at the creature. But it ducked, and the blade went whizzing past its head into a tree trunk.

'NICE TRY, GIRLY GUMDROPS,' grunted the ogre.

Betty wouldn't give up that easily. She sprang to her feet – though her bottom still hurt abominably – and lifted her sword. 'Come on, then, Grot Boy, do your worst!' she cried.

Like two oddly matched dancing partners, the girl and the ogre edged towards each other in perfect fighting poses. Betty made her plan. *Dash forward. Lunge. Cartwheel. Backflip. Then strike the beast.* POP GOES THE WEASEL!

But, just as she was about to pounce, Betty felt something wobble under her feet. Before she knew it, the ground suddenly gave way. As leaves fell around her, she plummeted downwards, into a deep hole.

It was a trap.

Laughter echoed above. Strangely, it didn't sound like the ogre. Betty squinted in the light and could just make out someone peering down at her. Whoever this odd bod was, she stood upright

and tall like a human, but her skin was green and warty. Her pointy hat cast a shadow over two huge, bulging eyes – and her slimy green mouth turned down at the sides like a disgruntled cucumber. Her wand, which was pointed straight at Betty, was made of stinging nettles and thorny vines.

Betty grew pale. It couldn't be the most gruesome enemy of the kingdom, could it? The one she'd chased away from the castle many moons ago?

'Oh yes . . .' the stranger said. 'It is I. The most gruesome enemy of the kingdom. The one you chased away from the castle many moons ago.'

Betty gasped. 'The Toad Witch!'

With an ear-splitting cackle, the Toad Witch pointed her thorny wand at Betty. 'CROAKUS POCUS!' she cried.

A puff of smoke engulfed the defenceless Guardian of Wobbly Rock. Betty felt herself seized by a strange force, her limbs flailing like hypnotised snakes. Somewhere, she could hear Figg's voice

calling out, but she was lost in a flurry of swirly-whirly zigzags. Her skin tightened. Her bones drew inwards. She felt like a raisin shrivelling in the sun.

Then – just as she wondered if she'd ever play *pin the wig on the weasel* again – everything went dark.

Chapter 4

 he Toad Witch lived beyond the forest at the edge of a pond. Her house was an enormous, upturned shopping trolley, the height of one and a half fish and chip shops, that had once belonged to a monstrous giant. She had dredged it up from the water with her magic some years before.

At the very back of her lair, where the cauldrons bubbled and the potions squeaked, the Toad Witch sat on her reclining toadstool and congratulated

herself on being such a massive genius. 'Never, in the history of toadkind, has anyone been such a massive genius,' she exclaimed. 'The Guardian of Wobbly Rock is mine, ALL MINE!'

Hearing the witch's croaky voice, Betty stirred and opened her eyes. 'What happened?' she whispered. 'Am I alive? **HAVE I MISSED AFTERNOON TEA?'**

The Toad Witch clapped her hands in excitement. 'Oh, goodie. You're awake!'

Betty looked around – and realised she'd been locked in a cage. More precisely, a birdcage, hanging from the top of the shopping trolley. There was no sign of Simon Anderson or Figg. She hoped they'd escaped unharmed.

'Let me out of here, Toady!' Betty said, with a scowl.

'Oh, you're not going anywhere.' The Toad Witch pulled a grin wider than an oven door. 'Gosh, I'm so clever. They said no one could defeat you, but I

knew my plan would lure you out. Only someone as arrogant as you would try to face an ogre on your own. And now, you're my prisoner.'

'Just wait till I get my hands on you!' Betty cried.

The Toad Witch let out a laugh like a car horn. 'You've not realised yet, have you? Oh, this is too good. It's so much fun being ridiculously intelligent!' She stood up and moved towards Betty's cage, her flat feet splatting on the muddy ground.

Betty frowned. Something didn't feel right. The Toad Witch looked oddly large . . . and, as she got closer, seemed to loom over Betty like a giant.

'Why are you so huge?' asked Betty, her heart beating quicker than a bongo player on fast-forward.

The Toad Witch put her bloated eyes up to the bars. 'The question is, why are YOU so SMALL?' she cackled.

Betty's belly did a triple somersault. 'Me?

Small?!' She looked down at her hands. At first, they seemed fairly normal. But when she held them up, she realised they were barely as big as the Toad Witch's nostrils. **'WHAT HAVE YOU DONE TO ME, YOU SLIMY SNOTTER?'** she shouted.

The Toad Witch smirked. 'Not so big and strong any more, are you?'

'You shrank me?!' Betty gasped. Her clothes, thankfully, still fitted, but her precious sword was nowhere to be seen. She tried to pummel the Toad Witch through the bars but the meanie simply rolled her eyes and stepped away.

'A simple incantation, really,' she said smugly.

Betty shook the cage. 'Change me back **NOW!** I'm Betty Steady. I'm supposed to be tall. I'm supposed to be powerful and amazing.' She slapped her tiny forehead with her tiny hands. 'Oh, this can't be happening! This has got to be a dream. **WAKE UP, BETTY. WAAAAKKKE UP!'**

'Tough luck, sweetie. This is real life.' The Toad Witch poured herself a gloopy purple drink from a potion bottle. 'Life isn't always a picnic. It's not a barn dance either. Or a school trip to the adventure park. Nope. Life is hard, and things change.' She took a big gulp of her drink. 'Take me, for instance.

There was a time when my family was rich and powerful. I lived in a castle. I had luxuries just like you grubby humans in Wobbly Rock. Banquets and balls and table tennis. Life was perfect.'

'I don't give a flying fish knife about your life!' Betty tried to calm herself down. To assess her situation. How could she get out of here?

'Then one day, everything changed.' The Toad Witch clutched the side of the trolley and gazed out over the pond. 'My father gambled our fortune on a high-stakes game of snakes and ladders. He lost everything on one roll of the dice. And in that moment, I promised myself one thing. I would get that life back some day. That – little Betty – is why I intend to take Wobbly Rock for myself. And unlike last time, I will succeed.'

'NO!' cried Betty. 'I won't let you.'

'I'm afraid you don't have a choice, pipsqueak.' The Toad Witch cracked a horrid smile. 'With you locked away here, I'm free to set my terrifying army

on your precious home once more. And this time, King Nutmeg and his knights won't be able to stop me, not without their secret weapon . . . you! Wow, it's exhausting being this brilliant.'

But before the Toad Witch could continue explaining her devilish plan, a voice piped up from outside.

'MUUUUUUUUUUUUUUM?'

The Toad Witch tutted. 'What, Nim?' she said. 'I'm busy.'

A teenage toad with gangly arms climbed inside the trolley. 'MUUUUUM!' he moaned. 'I'm so hungry, I could eat a climbing frame.'

'There's half a fish pie left over.' The Toad Witch

straightened her hat and signalled to her son that Betty was there. 'Now, keep it down. We have a guest.'

'MUUUUUUUUUM. I hate fish pie! You KNOW I don't care about this evil witch stuff. You're so embarrassing.'

'Don't be rude,' said the Toad Witch. 'Don't you want to live in a castle?'

Nim shrugged. 'Who even cares?'

The Toad Witch's eyes bulged more than ever. 'I do! When my army attacks Wobbly Rock in two days' time, I'll be the queen of the castle. And boring King Nutmeg will be the dirty old rascal.'

In her birdcage, Betty fell to her knees. In two days all her pals were going to be toad food, and there was nothing she could do to stop it. Poor Pam and Pamm! Poor Lady Mayfly and Sir Loin of Beef! Poor Johnny Logflume and his dazzling flag! Oh, it was more than she could bear.

The Toad Witch cracked her slimy knuckles. 'Now,

it's time to summon my underlings.'

Her son groaned. 'Ugh, Mum! They're well annoying!'

But the Toad Witch ignored him, held her spiky weed wand skywards and looked up at the clouds. In a voice as loud as five bagpipes, she cried, 'CREATURES OF SLIME AND GRIME AND SIN. HEAR MY CALL AND GATHER HERE.'

'Are you joking?' said Nim. 'That doesn't even rhyme.'

The Toad Witch blinked. 'You what?'

'What kind of witch doesn't rhyme her spells?' said Nim. 'You are so sad.'

The Toad Witch sighed and held her wand up again. 'CREATURES OF SLIME AND GRIME AND SIN, HEAR MY CALL AND GATHER . . . OVER THERE . . . BY THAT BIN.'

Nim put his head in his hands. 'Give me strength.'

Despite the stinky poetry, the Toad Witch's spell somehow worked. As the sky darkened with clouds,

Betty could feel a rumbling underground. Soon,
a mass of worms began to emerge from the earth
and slither towards the trolley – some small and
wriggly, others huge with razor blade teeth. Then
from the pond, a legion of frogs and toads, dripping
wet and slippery, crawled out and crept through
the trolley bars. From the darkness, two enormous
toads trudged into view, each as big as a tractor.
Last to join was the gruesome ogre from the forest.

Betty shuddered.

The Toad Witch stood before her kitchen
bin (which really needed emptying) and
looked out at her terrifying army.
She pushed back her shoulders,

taking in the glorious stench. Good golly, she felt powerful.

'My faithful followers, the time has finally come to storm Wobbly Rock!' she croaked.

'Bring your arrows and swords. Bring your daggers and axes. And if anyone needs the toilet, please go before we leave. It's a long journey and I don't want to be stopping every five minutes.'

Betty rattled the cage and yelled, but no one could hear her above the cries of the terrifying army. As the hordes followed the Toad Witch into the forest, she could see Nim trailing at the back, moodily kicking a stone.

When they'd all disappeared into the distance, Betty tried desperately to pull apart the bars of the birdcage. 'Ugh,' she cried. 'I hate being so weak and small and useless.'

There was nothing she could do. All was hopeless. All was lost.

And then – as the wind blew through the trees – an enchanted boiled egg sang a song about a nice rainbow.

Hang on . . . sorry. Salvador Catflap here. That's actually part of a completely different book I've been writing called *The Enchanted Boiled Egg and the Nice Rainbow*. (A really serious and important story about love and loss which I'm expecting to win some sort of fancy award.)

I can only apologise for the interruption. Back to Betty's story . . .

Betty, scared and alone, heard a sudden jangling sound. She peered anxiously down through the birdcage bars – to see none other than Figg, sitting on the witch's toadstool, holding a set of keys.

Figg smiled. 'I slipped these out of the Toad Witch's pocket. Not bad for someone with the strength and courage of a dishcloth, eh?'

Betty had never been so happy to see the little green nuisance in all her life.

nce Figg had emptied the Toad Witch's bin and taken the bag out (hygiene was hygiene after all, and Tuesday was bin day) he set about freeing Betty. He climbed to the top of the shopping trolley, shimmied down the rope which held the birdcage and unlocked the cage door. As Betty climbed out, they both realised Figg was a bit taller than her.

Betty gave a snort of disbelief. 'This has got

to be a joke! You're TINY, which means at the absolute most, I'm the height of two Jammie Dodgers.' She looked up at the sky and cried, **'OH, HEAVENLY HANDS OF FATE, WHY DID YOU HAVE TO MAKE ME SMALLER THAN THE IMP?!'**

'Careful,' said Figg. 'I could lock you up again if I wanted to.'

'Forget that.' Betty held Figg by the ears and stared straight in his eyes. 'We need to hurry! That toad is headed for the castle. We must save our friends – and get the witch to change me back to my normal size. Now, where's Simon Anderson?'

'Ahhh,' said Figg. 'I'm afraid your faithful stallion scarpered.'

Betty scowled. Had her magnificent horse taken one look at her pathetic new stature and run off in shame? Nonsense, she told herself. She WASN'T pathetic. She was still the Guardian of Wobbly Rock, the best fighter in the whole kingdom.

'I don't need a horse!' she said out loud. 'And I don't need a sword either. I'VE GOT BARE FISTS AND A CAN-DO ATTITUDE! Come on, Figg! Let's get out of here.'

Nearly three hours later

'I CAN'T DO this,' said Betty, traipsing through the mud. 'My feet hurt and I'm tired.'

Though they'd been walking for nearly three hours, they'd only covered a small section of the forest. It felt strange, being so little. Every pebble looked as big as a boulder, every twig was like a fallen tree, and every leaf looked like a really massive leaf.

When Betty couldn't take any more, she took a seat on an acorn.

'No stopping,' said Figg. 'If we're going to catch up with the Toad Witch, we need to keep going.'

'Surely there's an easier way.' Betty thought for a while, then jumped up. 'I've got it! We have to find a . . . a . . . Oh, what are they called again? The flappy feather things?'

Figg wondered if Betty had accidentally eaten a funny-looking mushroom. 'I beg your pardon?'

'You know,' said Betty. 'The beaky sky-people. The ones that look like hamsters, with wings.'

'Are you talking about birds, Betty?'

Betty clapped her hands. 'Yes! Birds!'

Figg nodded slowly. 'Come to think of it, that is an interesting idea.'

Betty grinned. 'Not so bad for someone with the IQ of a toilet brush, eh?'

Figg took out the paperwork from his waistcoat. 'There's an article in an old BUM that might help . . . Where was it? Cheese Triangle Regulations, no . . . Duck, Duck, Goose Safety Guidelines, no . . . Ah,

here we go, Bird Population of the Forest of Dust.'

Betty tapped her foot. 'Can't we just ask any bird?'

'Absolutely not,' said Figg. 'Preparation is key. It says here that the number of native wood pigeons has fallen in recent years . . .'

As Figg reeled off a snore-fest of facts, Betty zoned out and stared up at the trees. The world was terribly big now. How insignificant she felt, looking up at the mighty oaks, at the great leaves shadowing the sun, at the blackbird perched on the branch.

'BLACKBIRD!' she cried, leaping up. **'TICK TOCK! IT'S BLACKBIRD O'CLOCK!'**

'Wait, Betty!' shouted Figg.

But it was too late. Betty was already climbing the tree like a banana-crazed baboon.

'BLACKBIRD! BLACKBIRD! BLACKBIRD! BLACKBIRD!'
she cried.

Even though she was small, in no time Betty reached the branch and came face to face with the bird.

'**BLACKBIRD!**' she panted. 'You are one lucky beak-boy! For I am the great Guardian of Wobbly Rock!'

The bird ruffled his feathers. 'How nice for you.'

Betty beamed. 'And you, my friend, get to help me save the day!'

The blackbird rolled his eyes. 'Waiter, I'll take a plate of NO with a side order of LEAVE ME ALONE.'

Betty frowned. Had she heard him correctly? Who wouldn't want to team up with the greatest fighter known to humankind? 'But . . . but . . . I need to save the castle from the Toad Witch,' she said.

The blackbird scoffed. 'Darling, do you think I have nothing better to do than help a bunch of humans? Puh-lease.' He shuffled to the end of the branch. 'Entitled nitwits, the lot of you.'

Betty scrambled sombrely down to the ground. 'He was charming,' she told Figg.

Figg sighed and read an extract from his BUM. 'Blackbirds, pigeons and starlings harbour a deep distrust of humankind due to a long-standing netball club rivalry.'

'All right, Captain Know-It-All,' Betty grumbled. 'So which birds WILL help us?'

'Says here, the Great Thunder Owl is our best bet,' said Figg. 'Helpful, speedy and not particularly fussed about ball sports. There's only one of them remaining in these parts, though.'

'Great Thunder Owl?' said Betty. 'Where would a hot-shot hooter like that hang out?'

Figg smiled and tapped the page. 'And you say paperwork is useless?' He folded up the BUM and returned it to his waistcoat. 'We're going to the Tree-House Tavern. AND THE CHERRYADES ARE ON ME!'

And now . . . the part of every good story where our plucky heroes enter an alehouse only to be met with suspicion. Good golly gherkins, I can't wait!

I'm sure you can imagine the forest tavern vibe. A hedgehog playing the lute. Fairies with tankards of fizzy pop. Stick insects performing karaoke. Standard stuff.

Out of breath, having climbed the steps up the tree trunk, Betty and Figg burst through the tree-house door. As the room fell into ominous silence, all eyes turned to them. The fairies put down

their fizzy pops. The stick insects lowered their microphones. The hedgehog put his lute in his lute-shaped lute holder. Golly gherkins indeed!

'Do we smell?' whispered Figg.

Betty tried to whisper, but her voice could never quite resist shouting. 'I don't smell. I have armpits like a –'

'Yes, yes. A fresh meadow. I know.' Figg smiled awkwardly at the Tree-House Tavern customers. 'Now, where is that owl?'

'I doubt an owl could even fit its rear end in here,' said Betty. 'Let's just get on with it and ask someone.'

But as she took a step forward, a muscly fairy blocked her.

'Whadda you two want?' he growled. He had black wings, skulls on his bandana and a tattoo on his arm which said I HATE STRANGERS.

Betty summoned the confidence of a really cool person in leather trousers. 'I am the Guardian of

Wobbly Rock and I'm seeking the Great Thunder
Owl to take us to the castle!'

'Ain't no owl here.' The fairy flexed his muscles.
'Sling yer hook.'

Betty was NOT used to being spoken to like that.
'Pipe down, poser!' she snarled.

Figg tugged on her cloak. 'I wouldn't wind up the
locals, Betty.'

The fairy squared up to Betty. 'What did you call
me?'

'A massive **POSER.**' Betty clenched her fists and pulled back her shoulders, trying to pretend the fairy wasn't nearly double her size. 'You know what? This time yesterday I could have squashed you with my big toe.'

'Well, it ain't yesterday, is it?' sneered the fairy. 'And it ain't tomorrow either. (That's bin day.) It's today. And today, you don't scare me one bit.'

Betty swallowed down an extra-large, stuffed-crust slice of fear and reached for her sword. 'Blast,' she said, remembering she'd lost it. There was nothing else to do but hold up her fists and make a snarly face.

The fairy laughed. 'Wind yer neck in, love.'

'Scared to fight me, eh?' said Betty with a swagger. **'YEAH, I BET YOU ARE, BANDANA BRAIN!'**

She lunged forward and biffed the lairy fairy on the arm. It barely registered. What's more, it made her hand throb like a stubbed toe on a door frame.

66

The fairy smirked at his buddies who were cheering him on and took a slow sip of his fizzy pop.

'Betty, I suggest you back down,' said Figg. 'You're not quite the fighter you once were.'

But that wound Betty up even more. DOLLY-DOUBTERS, THE LOT OF 'EM! she thought.

At full speed, Betty ran towards the burly fairy, walloping head first into his chest. BOING! She bounced off, stumbled back and landed with a crash on top of the hedgehog's lute.

'My lute!' cried the hedgehog. 'Tickle my prickles, you'll pay for this! Come on, guys, let's get her!'

Betty scrambled to her feet as a throng of fairies and stick insects closed in. She steadied her breathing and made a plan. *Forward roll. Lunge. Backflip. Whack 'em all on the nose, one by one.* HOT CROSS BUNS!

But, as the creatures got closer, Betty shrank back. Somehow, she was no longer able to summon the strength of the trees . . . or the power of the

wind . . . In fact, she could barely summon the confidence of a really boring person in flannel pyjamas. With all her prowess shrivelling up, she curled into a ball and sucked her thumb.

Just when all was apparently lost, a figure suddenly leaped on to the bar. Betty looked up to see a field mouse in a bobble hat.

'STAND BACK!' the field mouse cried. Like a majestic flea, she jumped up and grabbed hold of the iron chandelier overhead, swinging towards Betty and seizing two flaming candles.

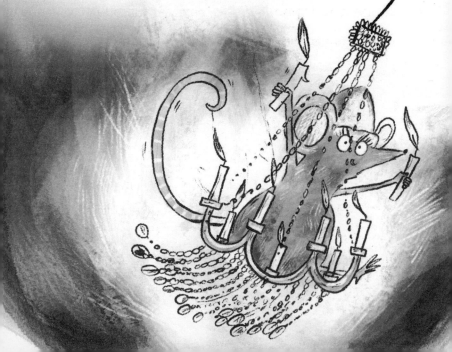

As she let go, the mouse landed on the floor in front of the angry gang and brandished the fire. 'GET AWAY FROM HER, YOU BUNCH O' BULLIES!'

'Or wot?' said the fairy.

'Or that'll be the last fizzy pop you ever drink!'

The muscly fairy thought for a moment, then shrugged. 'She ain't worth it.'

As everyone else backed away, the mouse turned to Betty with an overly intense grin. 'Wow!'

'Double wow!' replied Betty.

'She means, *thank you*,' said Figg.

'You're welcome,' said the mouse, helping Betty to her feet. 'Oh, and by the way . . . I think I know where your owl is.'

‘I WANT TO PLAY THE TRUMPET!' said the mouse, leading Betty and Figg into her underground hideaway.

'Fair enough,' said Betty, still feeling rubbish about how much of a wet wimp she'd been in the Tree-House Tavern. 'But what's that got to do with us?'

The mouse showed them inside a quaint little room, complete with a fireplace, a table set for tea and a wall full of trumpets. 'Take a seat,' she said,

lighting the fire and putting the kettle on. 'As you can see, trumpets are my life.'

'That's great,' said Betty, shifting in her armchair. 'Now, about that owl –'

'Ever since I was a young mouse, I've dreamed of being First Royal Trumpeter. You know – the person who goes DO-DO-DO-DO as the king or queen walks in.' The mouse sighed. 'Oh, what I wouldn't give to DO-DO-DO-DO all day long.'

'Everyone should have a dream,' said Figg. 'So . . . the Great Thunder Owl?'

'Imagine me, dressed in my finery, trumpet-to-mouth, tooting myself silly. Heaven.' The mouse sat on a stool next to Figg. 'Now, I have a plan . . .'

Figg narrowed his eyes. This mouse wanted something from them.

The mouse poured the tea. 'You want to find the Great Thunder Owl? Well, I can track him down for you – on one condition . . .' She paused dramatically. 'You let me come with you to the castle.'

Figg shook his head. 'No tag alongs, I'm afraid. It's too dangerous. We're heading straight into a fearsome frog fight.'

'Danger is my middle name!' The mouse stood

up with a look of determination in her eyes and a bag of custard creams under her hat. 'Biscuit, anyone?'

'Yum! Yes please,' said Betty. 'Wait . . . Your middle name is Danger?'

'Well, not really, no.' The mouse laid two custard creams on Betty's plate. 'But it might as well be. I'm pretty darn brave.'

'What *is* your name?' asked Figg, though he was mostly wondering when the biscuits were coming his way.

Proud as pudding, the mouse announced, 'Elle Emen-O'Pea.'

Figg wasn't sure if he'd heard her correctly. 'L M N O P?'

'Yes, Elle Emen-O'Pea.'

Figg put down his teacup. 'As in, Q R S T U V?'

The mouse blinked. 'Pardon?'

'Like the alphabet?' asked Betty.

'I don't know what you mean,' said Elle Emen-

O'Pea. 'I'm Elle. I come from a great line of Emen-O'Peas. What's confusing? Anyway . . . back to business.'

Figg and Betty shot each other a look which screamed, WEIRD, WEIRD, BUMBLE-BEE BEARD!

'Now,' said the mouse. 'You must take me to Wobbly Rock! For, it is there that I will finally fulfil my wildest dreams. To play trumpet for the king!'

'I'm not sure King Nutmeg has an opening for that position,' said Betty. 'But if you give me a copy of your CV, I can pass it on.'

Elle Emen-O'Pea gave her a stare icier than a slushy on a snow day. 'I SAVED YOUR BACON, MISSY. YOU OWE ME!'

The mouse had her there. Betty hated to think about how much of a sad sack she'd been. 'I suppose you're right,' she said.

'Look,' said Figg. 'If you agree to sign the risk assessment, follow proper battle rules and give me a custard cream, then we can take you to the castle.

But there are no guarantees that the king will let you stay.'

'Oh, just wait till he hears me!' said Elle Emen-O'Pea. 'HIS EARS WILL WEEP WITH JOY.'

And so it was settled. The mouse would get her wish. At dawn, she would lead Figg and Betty to the Great Thunder Owl himself. But, for now, they all needed a good rest. It had been a long day. And who knew what fresh challenges awaited them tomorrow?

After a hearty dinner of hot broth and curly fries, the mouse made her guests a bed of cushions and read them a bedtime story (the prequel to *The Enchanted Boiled Egg and the Nice Rainbow* called *Misery and Suffering* by none other than me, Salvador Catflap). Then she tucked them in and wished them goodnight.

Betty wasn't sure she'd be able to sleep, knowing that her dear friends were in danger – not to mention coming to terms with being weaker than orange squash made from the last dribble in the bottle. But she needn't have worried, because Elle Emen-O'Pea played them a gentle lullaby on the trumpet, called *Once Upon a Waffle*. It was so soothing and beautiful that Betty drifted into a deep slumber, dribbling peacefully down her chin.

igg tapped Betty on the shoulder. 'Wake up!' he whispered. 'You need to see this impressive BURP I've been working on.'

Betty rubbed her eyes. 'Excuse me?'

'My *Biannual Unabridged Rescue Plan*,' said Figg. 'I got up early and updated it, ready to save the castle.'

Betty turned over and buried her head into the pillow. 'UGH!' she groaned. 'For a minute, I'd

forgotten all about this waking nightmare. Not only am I miniscule – and the castle is in danger – but I'm stuck with an imp who's so dreary his best friend's probably a paper clip.'

'Hey!' said Figg. 'Henry is a very good listener.'

'Morning cupcakes!' sang Elle Emen-O'Pea, twirling into the living room. 'Make sure you get yourselves a good breakfast. WE'RE GOIN' OWL HUNTIN'!'

As the three tiny adventurers trekked the forest, with only half a pack of custard creams and a trumpet between them, the mouse explained the plan. The Great Thunder Owl, until recently, had nested on the roof of the Tree-House Tavern – but, in his old age, he'd grown irritated by the nightly karaoke. Rumour had it, he'd moved into a woodland retirement home. It wasn't far away, but they'd need to cross the river to get there.

'No sweat,' said Figg. 'I have my fifty metres swimming badge.'

'That won't help you around these parts,' said the mouse. 'Water's too rough. No. We've got to cross the Ol' Shaky Twig Bridge.'

Betty didn't like the sound of the Ol' Shaky Twig Bridge. And when she saw it for herself, she didn't like the look of it either. The twigs looked as though they'd been glued together by a three-year-old using a cheap glue stick – not the good stuff she looked after.

Betty trembled. Her heart hammered. Her belly made a strange gurgly noise, which sounded a bit like, OH, HEAVENLY HANDS OF FATE, IS THIS A JOKE?

You might be wondering why Betty was quite so afraid. Well, she'd never admitted it to Figg – but she couldn't swim.

'Is Nappy-Bum Baby scared?' Figg laughed and pinched Betty's cheeks. 'Don't worry. I'll protect you.'

'I am NOT a Nappy-Bum Baby,' Betty said.

But as she stepped on to the precarious bridge, the truth was . . . she felt like the world's wimpiest baby wearing the world's wettest nappy. With each slow shuffle forward, Betty had to will herself on. *Do this for Pam. Do this for Pamm. Do this for Johnny Logflume and his exceptional flagmanship.*

'This bridge is in urgent need of a safety inspection,' said Figg. (Even when crossing dangerous waters he was duller than a concrete museum.)

Betty was barely halfway across when she made the mistake of looking down at the white rapids. One wrong move and she'd get a one-way ticket to Splash City.

CRACK! A twig suddenly snapped under Elle Emen-O'Pea. The mouse fell, legs dangling over the river.

'HELP!' the mouse cried, clinging to the bridge with one paw and holding tight to her trumpet with the other. 'I MUST LIVE TO TOOT ANOTHER DAY!'

In that moment, Betty shook off her fear like a wet dog. She was the Guardian of Wobbly Rock and a life was in danger!

'WORRY NOT, MOUSEY!' she cried. **'YOU'LL TRUMPET AGAIN!'** She leaped across the twigs and knelt by the dangling mouse. Ignoring the spray of angry water, she grabbed Elle's paw. 'GOT YA,' she said, heaving with every ounce of strength she could muster.

'I'm slipping!' cried the mouse.

Betty held tight and pulled hard. **'COME ON, LINDA AND GREGG! DO YOUR THING!'**

Linda and Gregg were Betty's biceps. And even though they were smaller than they once were, they were no less loyal. They'd been there for her through thick and thin. Through long-sleeved

blouses and winter coats. And now it was their time to shine once more. Betty strained. Her arms shook with the weight but Linda and Gregg were tough. With an enormous yank and an even more enormous grunt Betty dragged Elle Emen-O'Pea on to the bridge.

'Wow!' said Betty, gasping for breath and thankful she was still fabulous.

'Double wow!' said the mouse.

The Compost Heap was a retirement home for woodland creatures, set in a mound on top of the riverbank. Staffed by a team of squirrels, it offered a retreat to forest folk who needed a bit of extra TLC in their twilight years.

The Great Thunder Owl, whose full name was Rupert Sometimes, liked to spend Tuesday mornings in the sunroom, gazing out at the garden. This way he could enjoy his black coffee and

crossword while waiting for the bin men. There was nothing he liked more than to watch the trash bags get slung into the back of the rubbish cart: banana skins tumbling, baked beans oozing. Bliss.

So when Betty, Figg and Elle Emen-O'Pea came trundling into the Compost Heap to see him, Rupert Sometimes was not in the mood to be disturbed.

'ANY DAY BUT BIN DAY!' he said, with his grey feathers standing on end.

'I thought he was supposed to be friendly,' whispered Figg.

'We need to save the castle!' said Betty. 'You're our only hope.'

Rupert Sometimes pushed his spectacles up his beak. 'The only thing I need to do is solve these last three crossword clues and wait for the sound of the rubbish cart.'

'Crossword?' Figg did a little jig before making himself comfortable on the armchair next to the

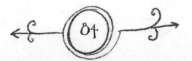

84

owl. 'I'm your imp. Crosswords are my thing.'

The owl, who was almost double the height of the imp, peered down. 'Oh, really? This one is a toughie, you know.'

'Try me, owl.' Figg put his hands behind his head and his feet on the coffee table, before realising it was unsanitary and taking them off again.

Rupert Sometimes picked up his newspaper (pretending to be irritated, but secretly ecstatic to have found a fellow crossword nut). 'Six down,' he said. 'Traditionally, the Fifth Royal Chef prepares which delicacy?'

Figg smirked and adjusted his waistcoat. 'Easy. *Pickled onions.*'

The owl was impressed. 'All right. Nine across. What is the most effective method to remove weeds from a royal garden?'

Figg scoffed. '*The Two-Step Tickle.* First, tickle the weed with a large feather. Then, in a firm voice, tell it to BOG OFF! Works every time. I thought these

85

were supposed to be hard?'

Rupert Sometimes smiled. 'Cor blimey! You are good! OK, last one . . .'

By now, everyone in the room was watching, including two elderly rabbits halfway through a game of Twister and a squirrel wiping up a large brown stain on the carpet.

'Twelve across,' said the owl. 'What is the most delicious expression of disbelief?'

Figg wrinkled his eyebrows. 'How many letters?'

'Seven and five.'

'*Baloney*? No, that doesn't fit.' Figg loosened his collar. '*Nonsense noodles*? No, that's not it either.' He'd never been this stumped on a crossword clue.

'Come on,' urged Elle Emen-O'Pea.

'I CAN'T DO IT!' cried Figg, crumbling under the weight of the pressure.

Betty wasn't having any of it. 'Oh, twaddle cakes, imp!' she said. 'You can do it. Just think!'

'That's it!' said Figg, leaping from the chair. 'TWADDLE CAKES. A delicious expression of disbelief.'

'I . . . I got it?' said Betty. The imp nodded.

'I GOT IT! TWADDLE CAKES!'

As Betty, Figg and the mouse joined hands and sang *Ring a Ring o' Roses*, Rupert Sometimes shook his head. 'Well, I never,' he said. 'What a bunch of champions. I guess I better help you after all.'

Betty's mouth fell open. 'Holy hula hoops! You'll help us?'

The owl nodded. 'Too right I will. I can take you

as far as the Noxious Valley of the Snails AND NO FURTHER. But first . . .' He pointed out of the window to the rubbish cart pulling up.

And so there in the sunroom, as our heroes cuddled up together and ate custard creams, they watched a dance as old as time itself – the ever-captivating *Collection of the Bins*. Sometimes life really was beautiful.

etty clung to the owl's feathers as they soared over the treetops. Boy, this owl was fast! In the distance, she could see all the way to Mount Crumbledown, where the castle stood high and mighty, like a gorilla in a hot-air balloon.

'Enemy to the left,' shouted Figg, pointing to the shadowy mass that was the terrifying army of the Toad Witch. 'They're heading south-south-south-south-south-south-south-south-south-south-west,

to the base of the mountain. They'll be there by
morning.'

Betty squinted in the wind and spotted the
scoundrels far ahead, moving together like a gang
of angry peas. Those toady whatnames were going
to rue the day they messed with the Guardian of
Wobbly Rock! At this speed, she was sure the owl
would catch up with them by nightfall. But, when
the bird began to slow down, and Betty's view of the

enemy was suddenly obscured by trees, she wasn't so sure after all.

'We're landing,' cried Elle Emen-O'Pea, cradling the trumpet to her chest like a curly brass baby.

'Already?' shouted Betty. 'But we're still far behind the Toad Witch!'

Nevertheless, Rupert Sometimes continued his descent before the edge of the forest, where the Noxious Valley of the Snails stretched before them. Betty gripped tight as they landed with a bump on the glittery forest floor. (A note about pixie dust: most people assume pixies scatter their sparkly powder using some kind of elaborate magic dance. But, in actual fact, the dust is mostly just pixie dandruff. Those little creatures really do suffer with flaky scalps.)

'This is as far as I'll go,' said the owl, with a wistful look in his eyes that yelled, THERE'S SOMETHING I'M NOT TELLING YOU.

'Why can't you take us all the way to the castle?'

said Betty as a pixie flew past, scratching its head. 'There's something you're not telling us.'

As the three adventurers clambered down to the glistening grass, the owl sighed. 'Too right there is.'

Figg looked up to his old friend – whom he'd known at least an hour – and held the end of his wing. 'Let it all out, buddy,' he said. 'We're the Crossword Crew. Loyal to the core.'

Rupert Sometimes nodded in agreement. They sure were. 'All right. I've never told anyone before, but I'm pretty sure I can trust you guys not to laugh at me. We've been through so much.'

Betty took his other wing and made a circle with Elle Emen-O'Pea. The old gang. The Awesome Foursome. 'We'd never laugh at you,' she said.

The owl took a deep breath. 'The truth is, I'm a Nappy-Bum Baby who's too scared to leave the Forest of Dust.'

'Oh, Rupert,' said Elle Emen-O'Pea. 'It's OK to be scared.'

93

Betty shook her head. 'Twaddle cakes!' she said. 'Being scared is for LUMPY LOSERS. We need a job doing and we need it doing now! So why don't you try closing your eyes and summoning the confidence of a really cool falcon in a leotard? Then you can take us all the way to Wobbly Rock.'

Elle Emen-O'Pea gave her a funny look. 'He doesn't have to do anything he doesn't want to.'

'But, if he just –'

The mouse took her trumpet and blew a long, flat note, like a gassy walrus. It shut Betty up, no mistake.

'Oh, I'm a big, wet blanket!' wailed the owl. 'I'll never be brave enough to leave. No way! No how!'

'You're no wet blanket,' said the mouse. 'You've helped us get so far!'

'I suppose you're right.' The owl smiled. 'We'll always have the memories we made along the way, won't we? Twaddle cakes! Custard creams! Beautiful bins! Oh, my friends. It's been wonderful, hasn't it?'

'Indeed, it has, pal,' said Figg. 'Indeed, it has.'

As Rupert Sometimes flew away, the three travellers watched in awe as his silvery feathers shone in the morning sun. Just as he was nearly out of view, they heard him call out, 'Smell you later!'

WHAT A SPECIMEN. AN OLD-TIME GENTLEMAN OF AN OWL. A REAL CLASS ACT.

Betty turned her attention to the Noxious Valley of the Snails ahead. This poisonous wasteland, bordered by wild hedgerows, was now the only obstacle standing between our heroes and Mount Crumbledown. Travelling around the edge of this toxic terrain (like clever Simon Anderson had done on the way here) would take far too long. Nope. The only way was straight through. How hard could it possibly be?

'Let's get groovin' then,' said Betty, heading straight for the field of sizzling grass.

'Hold your hamburgers!' said Figg. 'What part of *noxious* don't you understand?'

Betty slapped her forehead. 'Why is nothing simple?'

'Well, if you'd taken the time to glance at my BUM a few weeks ago, you'd have seen my analysis of the toxic grass,' said Figg. 'We can't risk trampling through it, unless we want our toes sizzled off.'

Betty felt like an erupting volcano. 'Listen up, Sally Sunshine. **I DON'T NEED NO STINKING TOES!'**

Figg sighed and pulled a sheet of paper from his waistcoat. 'If my map is accurate, then the little market town of Brown Smudge should lie just on the other side of this hedge. We can catch ourselves an old-fashioned snail ride!'

And now . . . the part of every good story, where our beloved heroes visit a little insect town only to be met with suspicion. Good golly gherkins, I can't wait!

I'm sure you can imagine the bug market vibe. Caterpillars selling dressing gowns. A wasp giving shoulder massages. A ladybird with a taco cart. Standard stuff.

Betty, Figg and Elle Emen-O'Pea rounded the corner of Brown Smudge to see a cluster of stalls lining the edge of a bog. As the market fell into ominous silence, all eyes turned to them. The caterpillars put aside their dressing gowns. The wasp paused mid-massage. The ladybird put her tacos in her taco-shaped taco suitcase. Golly gherkins indeed!

'Right,' said Figg. 'Time to find ourselves an old-fashioned snail ride!'

Betty didn't have the patience to be faffing around, so she strode straight up to the caterpillar stall.

'GOOD DAY, WRIGGLERS!' she said. 'WHERE ARE YOUR SNAILS AT?'

On closer inspection, the caterpillars' selection

of dressing gowns was quite exceptional and she rather fancied trying on a fluffy yellow one with FEELIN' LAZY on the back.

'I beg your pardon?' replied a blue caterpillar, with a river of mistrust in his eyes.

Figg said, 'We're looking for an old-fashioned snail ride!'

'That's not even a thing,' said the caterpillar.

'It is too!' said Figg, reminding himself that caterpillars were better known for their fabulous dressing gowns than for their intellect. (And he had to admit, he did like the look of one particular polka-dot robe.)

'Just tell us where the snails are!' said Betty,

feeling the minutes whizz by like annoying mosquitos. 'We've got to stop the Toad Witch! And get her to change me back to a big, brilliant fighting machine.'

'Toad Witch?' The blue caterpillar sniffed. 'What's that mean old croaker done now?'

Betty peered into the caterpillar's eyes, watching the river of mistrust evaporate into a cloud of curiosity. 'She's marching to Wobbly Rock, ready to attack the castle. But don't you worry. We're gonna get her!'

'That oily wretch! She's the worst.' The caterpillar beckoned Betty closer and whispered, 'All right, listen up. The snails have a taxi rank up past the grasshoppers' croissant stand. Tell 'em Mickey sent you.'

'Great,' said Betty. 'Who's Mickey?'

The caterpillar gave her a look that said YOU'VE GOT THE IQ OF A TOILET BRUSH and inched away.

The taxi rank was operated from an empty egg box at the dodgy end of the market. Owned by a silly old snail called Aunt Goggins, who had a shell like a walnut whip and eyes like Christmas morning, this business had been a beloved part of Brown Smudge for many a year. Every day, her loyal band of snails ferried travellers back and forth across the valley for the standard price of one lasagne each

way. No more. No less.

Oh, how the snails adored their profession! A fresh supply of lasagnes for a comfortable job. Snail slime, you see, could withstand the poison of the Noxious Valley of the Snails. Even the really bad poison that smelled like burnt crumpets. And what's more, the snails loved to spend their days ranting to their passengers – usually about how the fields were going to be turned into a mini-golf course, which wasn't at all true, but they liked having something to moan about.

Once our heroes had located the taxi rank, Figg strolled up to Aunt Goggins, cocky as a disco ball. 'We're in the market for an old-fashioned snail ride!' he declared.

'That's not even a thing,' said Aunt Goggins.

'Well, just a normal snail ride then,' said Figg. 'Mickey sent us.'

Aunt Goggins checked her notepad. 'For three of you?' She thought very hard and did some

complicated multiplication. 'That'll be three lasagnes.'

Figg checked his pockets. 'Blast! I left my purse back at the castle!'

'Can we pay you back?' asked Betty. 'We're kinda late for a battle with a Toad Witch!'

'No can do, little girl,' said Aunt Goggins. 'One lasagne each way. No more. No less. Come back when you can pay.' The snail turned away and began humming to herself while wiping up lasagne juice.

Elle Emen-O'Pea's ears pricked up. 'I recognise that tune!'

The snail smiled at the mouse. 'It's my absolute favourite song in the world!' she said. '*Once Upon a Waffle*. What a classic. Reminds me of summer evenings in the forest dance hall, sipping fizzy pop and holding hands with an earwig called Dave. Oh, those were the good old days!'

The mouse had an idea. She held her trumpet aloft like a royal lion cub. 'BEHOLD MY WIND

INSTRUMENT!'

Aunt Goggins beheld the wind instrument.

The mouse ran her hands over the trumpet in a very persuasive way. 'What say you to a once-in-a-lifetime trumpet performance of *Once Upon a Waffle*? In exchange for a ride across the valley?'

Aunt Goggins thought very hard and did some more complicated multiplication. 'I say, that's worth three lasagnes! No more. No less,' she said. 'IT'S A DEAL, MOUSEY!'

 *nce Upon a Waffle* carried across the valley like an empty crisp packet on the wind. Oh, how I wish I could describe how magnificent it sounded. Sure, you may have pleasant music in your world, but nothing you've ever heard can compare to the rousing melody shooting out of that little mouse's horn.

As Elle Emen-O'Pea tooted with every millilitre of lung capacity she could muster, she felt as

though she was at one with her trumpet. By the time the song came to a rousing and abrupt end, Aunt Goggins' mind had indeed travelled back to that glorious dance hall. She could taste the fizzy pop. She could feel the clammy touch of Dave the earwig's hands. 'Well, I'll be a monkey's mailman!' she said, her ears weeping with joy. 'That was fabulous.'

'Can we get a ride then?' asked Betty, impatiently.

Aunt Goggins turned to Elle Emen-O'Pea. 'You've given an old snail a little slice of memory pie. And it tasted mighty sweet. I'd be happy to oblige.'

'RIGHT THEN.' Betty snapped a twig from a bush and held it like a sword. 'TO THE CASTLE!'

Aunt Goggins looked Betty up and down with her wobbly tentacle eyes. 'You're going into battle like THAT?'

Betty peered down at her clothes. Flashy red tunic. *Check.* Floaty, mysterious cloak. *Check.* Boots with pointy toes for poking enemy shins. *Check.* She looked darn fabulous, despite being the size of a jacket potato. **WHAT WAS THAT SILLY SNAIL ON ABOUT?**

'One shot with an arrow and you'll be toast!' said the snail. 'Or worse – hash brown.'

'Oh.' Betty realised what she meant.

'Us snails come with armour.' Aunt Goggins

wiggled her shell. 'But you'll need your own if you're going to defeat that grotty gang of baddies.'

'Listen up, Sally Sunshine. **I DON'T NEED NO** –' Betty paused, rubbing her sore rear end, remembering her grapefruit-spoon injury. Maybe a little armour wouldn't hurt after all.

'Here,' said Aunt Goggins, finding a piece of old eggshell behind the egg box. 'Try this.'

The snail helped Betty and her friends fashion makeshift suits of armour consisting of half an eggshell in front and half at the back, tied together with string. It wasn't perfect – and smelled a bit funny – but it would protect them from toady snotbags, nonetheless.

When they were all ready, and armed with a selection of sharpened twigs, Aunt Goggins showed them to the holding pen at the side of the taxi rank, where a group of snails were waiting in the mud. 'Allow me to introduce your drivers for today,' she said. 'Betty, you'll ride on our fastest snail, the

incredible Teddy Whizzington. Elle Emen-O'Pea, you'll take our largest snail, the one and only Lola Flumpenhench. And Figg, you can have Keith. He has trapped wind.'

Betty hopped excitedly on to her snail and clung to his shell, looking out to the poisonous plains ahead. Elle Emen-O'Pea clambered on to her hefty snail, with her trumpet tucked under her arm. Figg eyed Keith with apprehension before climbing clumsily aboard, imp and snail both muttering *sorry* every few seconds.

Blimey, the Guardian of Wobbly Rock felt good.

Like her old self again, with a mighty sword and a speedy stallion. Taking a deep breath, she held her stick skywards and shouted at the top of her lungs, **'RIDE SWIFTLY, NOBLE SNAIL. LET'S GO LICK THE TOENAILS OF ADVENTURE!'**

After ten long minutes, the snails had travelled roughly seven centimetres.

Betty wanted to cry out to the HEAVENLY HANDS OF FATE in frustration, but she couldn't get a word in edgeways because Teddy Whizzington wouldn't stop going on about a stupid mini-golf course.

She glanced back to Figg, who – predictably – seemed to be riveted by his own snail Keith's dreary chat. 'Of course, planning permission for a mini-golf course wouldn't be easy,' she overheard him say. 'They'd need to fill in form thirty-six G, if I remember correctly.'

Betty groaned. This was not the hasty ride into battle she'd imagined.

'Don't worry,' said Teddy Whizzington. 'We'll speed up a bit once we hit the toxic sludge. Incidentally, that's where they're rumoured to be putting the second hole in the shape of a giant lobster.'

DON'T WORRY? Betty couldn't help but worry. In fact, she had a giant fluffball of worry strutting around her chest like an agitated alpaca. What if they were too late? What if King Nutmeg had to give up his throne to the Toad Witch? What if Sir Loin of Beef got biffed up by that ogre? What if Johnny Logflume's brilliant flag got chomped by a worm?

Elle Emen-O'Pea sensed Betty's unease, mostly because she'd said the majority of that last paragraph out loud. 'Relax, Betty,' she soothed. The mouse slid lower down Lola Flumpenhench's shell and leaned back with her arms behind her head. 'Snails are slow. That's life. Just enjoy the ride,

baby!' She began playing a laidback blues number on the trumpet.

Betty tried to tame the agitated alpaca within her heart. Every time she pictured Pam and Pamm coming face to face with a mean frog, she told herself it was OK – she still had time to save them. Snails were slow. That was life. She had to enjoy the ride, baby.

She got herself comfortable and pretended to listen to Teddy Whizzington, but really she was enjoying the music and the view. And the closer they got to the castle, the more grateful she felt that Wobbly Rock was her home. She loved every single one of those ridiculous courtiers. How she wished she could give them all a cupcake with YOU'RE SWELL written in pink icing.

As she watched the clouds fly by overhead, she wondered if her dear mother and father would have been proud of her. The HEAVENLY HANDS OF FATE had taken them away when she was so young, but she could still remember their sweet faces. Her mother's dark curls, her father's pigtails. They were great fighters too. Betty would never forget the last words her mother had spoken to her before they went riding off into that fateful battle. *My child*, she'd said, in a delicate whisper. *You've got jam on your chin.* And Betty had thanked her, for she did indeed have jam on her chin. Ahh . . . memories.

Betty suddenly sat up straight. Another memory had popped into her brain. All those years ago, after she'd wiped away the jam, her mother had said something else. What was it now?

Above the noxious valley, the sun shone through the clouds, as though the HEAVENLY HANDS OF FATE were trying to tell her something. Then it

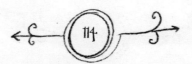

came to Betty like a hungry puppy. Her mother's final words . . .

Betty, you are so strong and powerful. But sometimes in life you'll need a little help, my Sally Sunshine.

A little help? A LITTLE HELP? She was the Guardian of Wobbly Rock. She didn't need no stinking help! Did she?

Betty thought very hard and did some complicated multiplication.

Then it hit her like a fridge door. She'd never have come this far without Figg or Elle Emen-O'Pea. Or Rupert Sometimes and the snails. Her mother was right. Maybe sometimes she did need some stinking help. And she was just about to ride into the biggest battle of her life! She needed more stinking help than ever!

She turned to Figg. 'Figg, can I see your **BUM** please?'

'Pardon me?'

'And your **BURP**. And the risk assessment.

I WANT TO READ IT ALL!'

'Good golly gherkins,' said Figg, smiling like a slice of Cheshire cheese. 'I never thought I'd see the day!'

By mid-afternoon they'd crossed half the valley, and Betty had brushed up on some SERIOUS paperwork. Yes, siree! Her brain felt like a stuffed mushroom, oozing with a perfect understanding of trip hazards and safety measures.

By early evening they'd made it to the final stretch of toxic grass and Betty had absorbed even more SERIOUS administration. Double yes, siree! Her heart felt like a festive stocking brimming with protocols and action plans.

By nightfall they'd finally reached the base of Mount Crumbledown and Betty had already forgotten half of what she'd read. But she could remember *some* of it. And *some* was better than *none* when it came to SERIOUS documents. Triple yes, siree! She felt pretty darn pleased with herself.

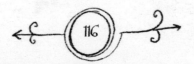

116

She looked up at Mount Crumbledown and cracked her knuckles. Those toads were for it now.

Chapter 10

 efore we come to the exciting climax of our story, there are three things you need to know. And, if you ask very nicely, I'll tell you.

Did you ask nicely? If you didn't, you can put this book down right now and lose five minutes of your playtime. But if you did ask nicely, well done. You can give yourself a pat on the left knee and read on.

ONE. The Toad Witch's army had made a camp halfway up Mount Crumbledown, out of view of the

castle. And they planned to attack at dawn.

TWO. Simon Anderson had arrived at the castle, dazed and confused, with weird sludge all over his cycling shorts. (I know what you're thinking. But he simply tripped over in a muddy bog. Get your brain out of the gutter, please.) Using a series of intricate hoof shuffles, he'd warned King Nutmeg that the Toad Witch was coming. Wobbly Rock was ready for the attack.

THREE. **The enchanted boiled egg asked his teacher if he could go to the toilet.**

Sorry . . . sorry. I've done it again, haven't I? I think you can guess what happened there. I'm a very busy author and sometimes I get my pieces of paper muddled up. Yesterday I accidentally wrote a letter to the bank on my living-room curtains. Let's try that last one again.

THREE. Betty, Figg and Elle Emen-O'Pea hid in a cave at the foot of Mount Crumbledown. As they finished off the last few crumbs of their custard creams, they came up with a brilliant plan.

Betty, with her new-found brain smarts, used a map, some local knowledge and a wet finger to find the perfect place for an old-fashioned ambush. (Which *was* a thing, unlike an old-fashioned snail ride, which definitely *wasn't*.)

The perfect place – she decided – was the Crag of Instability, a precipice overlooking the edge of the castle, high above the Toad Witch's army. But it couldn't be reached via the familiar mountain pathways. Instead, the route would be perilous and horrid. Figg wasn't sure they'd make it before first light, let alone whip up a risk assessment in time.

'I can climb **REAL** good!' boasted Betty. 'With Linda and Gregg on my side, I'll be up that mountain quicker than a skunk up a stepladder.'

Figg and Elle Emen-O'Pea weren't so sure at

first. But when they flexed their own bulging biceps they started to feel like maybe – just maybe – they could do this after all.

Reader, I want you to visualise what happened next. Imagine a little green imp, a field mouse with a trumpet and a tiny shrunken girl climbing a mountain with ease, swinging between holds like old pros, powerful and elegant as mini acrobats. Now, I want you to imagine the exact opposite of that. Because they were total rubbish.

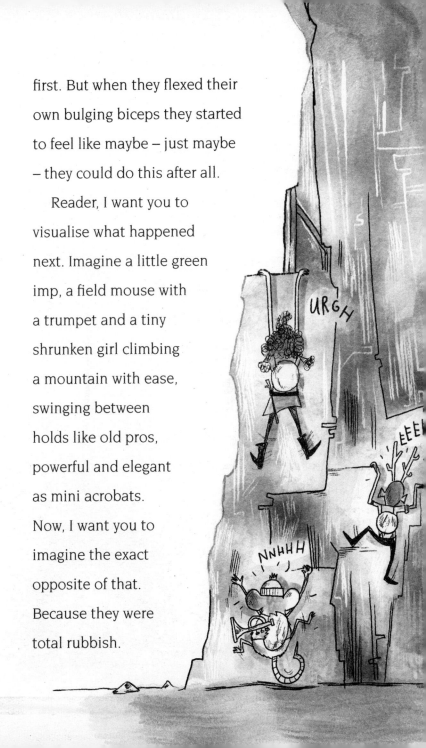

URGH

EEEE

NNHHH

Before long, our heroes were cowering on a windy cliff, hands throbbing, knees covered in cuts and bruises.

'Linda and Gregg,' cried Betty, flabbergasted. 'What's wrong with you today?'

'What's wrong with them?!' Figg shouted into the cold breeze. 'They're not used to climbing a GIGANTIC MOUNTAIN is what's wrong with them!'

'This was a stupid idea,' said Elle Emen-O'Pea. 'We're in serious danger and I'm calling for help!' She picked up her trusty instrument.

'NO!' said Betty. 'You'll give away our position!'

'But we're not going to be any help to the castle if we're stuck here like a gang of scaredy-pigs.' Ignoring Betty's protests, Elle blew her trumpet, long and clear. TOOT-TOOOOOOOT!

Betty put her head in her hands. She felt rotten.

How could she have let her people down so badly? Now, she'd never be able to get the Toad Witch to change her back.

SHE'D LICKED THE TOENAILS OF ADVENTURE ALL RIGHT, BUT IT TURNED OUT THOSE TOENAILS WERE COVERED IN FUNGUS.

Just as Betty was about to weep a river of sad sauce, a sound suddenly echoed across the mountain – a distant fluttering. Through the misty darkness, something bright emerged.

'What's that?' whispered Figg.

Like a silver netball of the night, a familiar owl sped through the sky.

'Rupert Sometimes!' exclaimed Elle Emen-O'Pea. 'You've come to save us!'

'My friends!' cried the owl. 'The Crossword Crew!'

'But I thought you were a Nappy-Bum Baby, too scared to leave the forest!' said Betty, grinning so hard, her cheeks nearly caught fire.

'I was!' said the owl. 'But when I got back to the Compost Heap and immediately started counting down the hours until bin day, I realised I was wasting my life! And I'd left behind the best pals I'd ever made.' He hooted with happiness and did a loop-the-loop in mid-air. 'And I remembered what you told me, Betty. *Close your eyes and summon the confidence of a really cool falcon in a leotard.* And I did it. Golly gherkins, I did it!'

'WE'RE SO PROUD OF YOU!' the others all said in perfect unison, as though they'd practised it at least thirteen times.

Rupert Sometimes landed gracefully on the rock. 'Hop on board, you utter gems. I'm taking you up the mountain! CROSSWORD CREW FOREVER!'

With the help of the exceptional owl, the gang were able to stop off at the castle to warn them about the impending attack. But to their surprise, Wobbly

Rock was ready and prepared for battle. Good old Simon Anderson. He's so DREAMY.

When King Nutmeg, Pam and Pamm caught sight of Betty, their eyes nearly popped out of their royal skulls.

'Great Guardian!' cried the king. 'What has that awful toad done to you?'

Pam and Pamm picked their friend up like a little dolly. 'Our best pal!' they whimpered.

'It's all right,' said Betty, realising that – actually – she'd rather got used to her new-found physique. 'I can still fight. I've got a wooden sword, eggy armour and a can-do attitude. Oh, and a wicked band of adventurers to help me!'

Pam and Pamm beamed with pride at their old buddy.

'Oh, and guess what?' said Betty. 'I'm real clever now. I did some **SERIOUS** reading and need to tell you some important informations.'

'Whoa!' said Pamm, so impressed that her bready crown quivered. 'You sound mad smart.'

Betty nodded wisely because her friend was spot on. 'Now, listen up. I studied Figg's BUM real hard and found a little-known fact about frogs and toads . . . *They hate vinegar*. Can't stand the stuff!'

'Yikes!' said Pam, turning to one of the guards. 'Tell the Fifth Royal Chef to throw out the pickled onions and bring up all the vinegar he can carry! Then send for the Royal Balloon Modeller, pronto. We're gonna make us some vinegar balloons!'

'You beauties!' said Figg. 'And good luck. We must leave you now and take up our position on the Crag of Instability. We've got some sneaky plans in store for those baddies.'

Betty hugged her princess pals and promised she would save them from the slimy wretch that was the Toad Witch. Then she waved goodbye to the knights and courtiers, who were busy funnelling vinegar into balloons at the battlements. And she gave a special wink to Sir Loin of Beef, Lady Mayfly and Margaret Fluff, as if to say **SORRY FOR BEING A BAG OF UNGRATEFUL UNDERPANTS.**

As the owl soared into the night sky, Betty watched Johnny Logflume's remarkable flag fade

into the distance in all its custard-yellow glory. This was it. Time to show that toad what the Guardian of Wobbly Rock could do.

Chapter 11

et yourself ready for a fearsome frog fight, boys and girls. Do up your seat belts, put on your top hats and enjoy the ride . . .

From her position on the Crag of Instability, Betty saw the army of the Toad Witch marching up the slope in all their soggy glory. Toads. Frogs. Worms. A snotty ogre. Nim trailing at the back, mumbling something about mountains being really boring.

Taking a deep breath, Betty did what she always did before a great battle. She closed her eyes and summoned the strength of the trees . . . the power of the wind . . . and – concentrating super hard – the confidence of a *whole disco* full of cool people in leather trousers. Oooooh-eeeee!

'KING NUTMEG!' cried the Toad Witch down below, riding on the back of a giant worm. 'YOUR BIG CHAIR IS MINE!'

Nim groaned. 'MUM, IT'S CALLED A THRONE! You're so awkward.'

The king looked out from the battlements and gulped. 'Not today, thank you.' But his voice was a bit nervy, and nobody could really hear him.

As the Toad Witch's army got into formation, the ogre broke forward and thumped on the castle door. Behind him, amphibians of all shapes and sizes were waiting with swords, spiky ball things and buckets of frogspawn. The two enormous toads loomed at the back, like a pair of giant, menacing potatoes.

The Toad Witch guided her worm towards the castle door and held up her thorny wand.

'CREATURES OF CRUELTY, I AM YOUR QUEEN! CAPTURE THE CASTLE AND . . . I MIGHT TREAT YOU ALL TO A NEW TRAMPOLINE.'

As you can imagine, Nim was cringing his webbed toes off.

King Nutmeg ordered the catapults to fire, but nobody could hear because his voice was all squeaky and scared. His daughters, however, were on top form and gave the command like two loud pelicans.

'FIRE!'

In an instant, a shower of vinegar balloons rained down over the villainous army, scattering

them all. Man, they hated vinegar so much!

Betty knew this was her best chance to strike that pesky ogre. But before she began, she reminded herself of the three rules of bamboozling a beast.

ONE. Approach from high ground. *Check*.

TWO. Stay upwind. *Check*.

THREE. Now, what was it again? Oh, yes . . . HAVE FUN! *Check-a-doodle-doo!*

She turned to Rupert Sometimes. 'Are you ready, old friend?'

The owl nodded. He was carrying a length of rope in his beak, which had been cleverly secured to the Crag of Instability. Using his new-found self-confidence, he soared down to the battlefield – dodging vinegar splats – and looped the string around a boulder. Job done! He felt super chuffed with himself and began pecking the nasty worms.

Betty held her stick over the rope and zip-lined down, remembering, of course, to have lots of fun. She biffed away a succession of toads with

her pointy boots and cried, **'EAT MY TINY TOES, YOU MEANIES!'**

Then, with a wallop, she landed just where she'd planned – looking up at the beastly ogre.

Betty quickly realised she was a LOT smaller than the last time she'd faced him. But, swallowing down a two-for-one multipack of fear, she made her plan. *Sneak up. Backflip. Clonk him on the back of the knee.* HEY DIDDLE DIDDLE!

Thanks to her clever plan –
and the fact that she was barely the
height of a toilet roll – it took a while for the
creature to even notice Betty was there. She crept
up until she was standing directly under him, then
backflipped like a pro. When the creature finally
spotted her, he flinched in disbelief.

'I DIDN'T WHIFF NO HUMAN!' (Good thing she'd
stayed upwind, eh?)

'Well, I can whiff you,' cried Betty, clonking him
on the back of the knee. **'AND YOU SMELL
LIKE DEFEAT.'**

He buckled and fell to the ground. 'I don't smell
like the feet. You do!'

'DEFEAT, silly!' shouted Betty. 'Yeesh,
you should do some **SERIOUS** reading and
get yourself some word-smarts.' She took her
sharpened twig and held it up to the ogre's face.
'Some of us have biceps *and* brains!'

But the ogre swiped Betty away with his big

sausage fingers, sending her flying into the mud. From here she could see the frogspawn launchers firing from the rear of the Toad Witch's army, blasting the castle with absolute goo (to her horror, some even landed on Johnny Logflume's lush flag). This spurred Betty on even more and she jumped to her feet, shouting, **'YOU HORRID LOT!'** With a great surge of anger she charged towards the ogre.

The beast grabbed his grapefruit spoon and proper lobbed it. But Betty was quick to dodge, letting it fall on the grass like a sad, loser spoon. Then the ogre picked up his dagger and jabbed all nasty like, but Betty stopped the blade with her sharpened twig, pushing with all her might.

Soon the dagger began to splinter the wood . . . but Betty used this to her advantage. When it snapped in two, she backflipped out of harm's way and threw the fractured ends at the ogre's eyes.

'AAARGH!' he cried. 'ME PEEPERS!'

When he fell to the ground in pain, she booted him in the behind, sending him rolling down the slope like a rancid rugby ball. Then she patted herself on the left knee for being an utter triumph.

By now, reader, you might be wondering what Figg and Elle Emen-O'Pea were up to. Well, I think they might have been playing *pin the wig on the weasel* or something, but I'm not sure.

Anyway, Betty turned her attention to the rest of the army and began bashing frogs and toads, left, right and centre.

HANG ON . . . I've just remembered Figg and Elle Emen-O'Pea weren't playing *pin the wig on the weasel* at all! They were doing cunning battle stuff.

From high on the precipice, the duo found they could throw vinegar directly on to the toad army without being spotted, so they soaked 'em good. And Figg, being a Billy Big-Brain, had a secret surprise tactic. It was a little-known fact that jazz music makes worms very confused and slither backwards. So he instructed Elle Emen-O'Pea to belt out some smooth tunes over the mountain, sending all the worms absolutely loopy.

Yes, siree! Wobbly Rock was showing those

invaders who was boss. But it wasn't over yet . . .

The Toad Witch jumped down from her jazz-crazed worm and held up her wand. 'CROAKUS POKUS!'

Two gigantic umbrellas whooshed out of the wand, like newborn lambs, and landed in front of the massive toads. The slimy pair were pleased as punch and used them to shield themselves from the oncoming vinegar as they began scaling the castle wall. (Slowly, of course, because they had to hold massive umbrellas.)

'Heaven's handkerchiefs!' cried Lady Mayfly, from the top of the castle.

'You can jolly say that again!' said Sir Loin of Beef, pouring as much vinegar down the wall as possible.

Margaret Fluff, the blacksmith, came bounding down the barricade with a big tub of paper clips. 'Quick. Chuck a loada these down!'

As luck would have it, Figg had ordered an extra-large box of paper clips for emergencies. Everyone

grabbed a handful and began hurling them at the umbrella-wielding nasties.

Margaret Fluff snatched one of the paper clips back from Lady Mayfly. 'Not that one!' she cried. 'That's Henry.' And she put him in her pocket for Figg.

But all the other paper clips were fair game and the people of Wobbly Rock tossed 'em at those toads like there was no tomorrow. It held them off for a while, but one of the toads was pretty nifty with the umbrella and managed to shield himself from the oncoming projectiles. It wasn't long before he'd managed to scramble to the top of the wall and on to the battlements.

Margaret Fluff and Sir Loin of Beef froze at the sight of the grotesque creature. But Lady Mayfly snapped into action, brandishing two knitting needles.

'COME ON THEN, WARTY, SHOW ME WHAT YOU GOT!' she cried.

Quicker than you can say *woolly jumper*, the toad shot out his sticky tongue and ripped the weapons from Lady Mayfly's hands. SLURP!

Margaret Fluff and Sir Loin of Beef were very protective of their dear friend and gave the toad a really dirty look. That'd teach him, no mistake! Then they remembered that amphibians weren't that bothered about dirty looks, so they got their swords out.

'JOLLY GET BACK, POND SCUM!' cried Sir Loin.

When the toad tried to shoot his tongue out again, Sir Loin and Margaret Fluff gave him a jab with their blades (and another dirty look, just because). The creature recoiled and stumbled into a wall just as Lady Mayfly smooshed a vinegar balloon in his face. SPLAT! He jumped away and plummeted down the castle wall, crying, 'VINEGAR IS THE WORST!'

Further along the castle, the other giant toad had finally made it up the wall. But luckily a gang of our

beloved characters was waiting! First, King Nutmeg clobbered it with a hockey stick. Then Pamm threw a handful of freshly cut bread. And finally, like an absolute master of kung fu, Johnny Logflume swirled his flagpole in the air, and shoved the toad into oblivion.

'I can't believe I just did that,' he said. 'I'd totally forgotten I could do kung fu.'

The Toad Witch looked at her dwindling army. 'Do I have to do everything myself?' she huffed. She raised her wand to the sky, preparing herself to cast another weird spell.

But tiny Betty appeared on the ground before the Toad Witch with her hands upon her hips.

'Listen up, Sally Snotslime,' she shouted. 'YOU AIN'T GETTIN' PAST ME.'

Chapter 12

'OU?' cried the Toad Witch, hardly believing her eyes. 'How did YOU get here?'

'With a loada help from me pals,' said Betty. 'Now, change me back and buzz off!'

The Toad Witch held up her spiky nettle wand and glowered like a really annoying customer demanding the manager. 'I'M NOT LEAVING UNTIL I GET A CASTLE! AND YOU CAN'T MAKE ME!'

Sitting on a boulder not far away, Nim rolled his

eyes. 'Hurry up, Mum. I'm sooooo tired.'

Betty brandished a pair of twig daggers. 'You ain't getting your warty hands on this castle!'

'CROAKUS POKUS!' A flash of blue shot from the Toad Witch's wand, but it bounced off Betty's eggy armour. (Good thing she was wearing it, eh?) As another shot exploded, Betty jumped out of the way with a triple somersault. She dodged the next with an excellent forward roll, then jabbed a twig dagger into the Toad Witch's webbed foot. THREE BAGS FULL!

The Toad Witch let out a scream as loud as three chickens on a roller coaster. 'GET OVER HERE AND HELP ME, NIM!' she shouted at her son.

'NO, MUM!' Nim groaned, unaware that Rupert Sometimes had landed behind him with Figg and Elle Emen-O'Pea on his back.

'We've talked about backchatting!' whispered the Toad Witch. When Betty plunged a second twig into her foot, she let out a scream as loud as three and a

half chickens on a roller coaster.

Betty wiggled her hips like a whole disco of cool people in leather trousers, did a few groovy dance moves, then full-on rugby-tackled the Toad Witch. Although the height difference made her look like a gerbil bashing against a patio door, Betty's strength was undeniable. With the help of Linda and Gregg, she floored the witch in seconds, pressing her pointy boots into her ribcage.

'NO ONE CAN DEFEAT THE GUARDIAN OF WOBBLY ROCK!'
Betty shouted.

The Toad Witch winced. 'AARGH!'

'Now, listen up,' said Betty. 'You're gonna change me back, then you're gonna leave Wobbly Rock and never return.'

'NIM!' cried the witch. 'GET OVER HERE!'

'Chill,' Nim tutted. But as he tried to take a step, he fell flat on his face (muttering an unrepeatable word) because his shoelaces had been tied

together. Behind him, Figg and Elle Emen-O'Pea gave each other a high five for being so brill.

'GRAB THOSE RASCALS!' cried the witch.

'But Muuum –'

'DO IT!' The witch gave Nim one of those special mum looks that means JUST WAIT TILL WE GET HOME.

Nim groaned again before dragging himself upright. Even though he was tied up like a terrible birthday present, he was large enough to outpace Figg and Elle Emen-O'Pea with a series of awkward jumps. Rupert Sometimes swooped down and tried to peck at him like an absolute hero but it was too late. That teenage toad picked up the imp and the field mouse with his soggy teenage hands.

'Hold 'em up so I can see,' said the Toad Witch. She smirked at Betty and produced her wand. 'How about I blast your precious pals into hundreds and thousands?'

Betty felt an entire buffet table of fear, which she

knew she'd never be able to swallow down. 'Please
. . .' she said, hardly able to breathe. 'Leave them
alone.'

The Toad Witch readied her wand, the nettles
twisting and sprouting like they were gonna do
something really naughty. Betty clenched her fists.
She had to find a way to save her chums. But how
could she stop the toad from firing another spell
from her weedy wand?

WEEDS! That was it! She clapped her hands. If she could destroy the wand of weeds and nettles, she could annihilate the witch's magic!

And – lucky as fudge – she remembered Figg had mentioned a way to destroy garden weeds during the crossword. What was it now? *The Three-Step Thrust*? No, that wasn't it. *The Seven-Step Shuffle*? No, not that either. Betty had to tap into some big-time brain smarts.

Think. Think. Think.

She thought harder than she'd ever thinked before. Then, as if from nowhere, the answer plopped into her brain like an unexpected teabag.

Of course. *The Two-Step Tickle*!

STEP ONE. Tickle the weed with a large feather.

Betty beckoned Rupert Sometimes over and yanked a feather from his wing. Then, before the witch even realised what was afoot, Betty gave the weedy wand a proper good ticklin'.

Before she moved on to STEP TWO, however,

something made Betty freeze.

If she destroyed the wand, then the Toad Witch would never be able to change her back. There would be no way of knowing if she could ever be the same old mighty Betty again.

Betty looked up at her friends' terrified faces. Sweet little Elle Emen-O'Pea, with her incredible trumpet. Sensible old Figg, with his trusty bumbag. (Oh, sorry, did I forget to tell you he always wore a bumbag? Whoops. I suggest you start this book all over again and imagine him wearing a really trendy bumbag the whole time. Or, alternatively, you can turn to page 161, where you'll find a whole page of bumbags to cut out and stick on to the pictures of our little imp friend.)

Betty shook her head. There was no way she could let the witch hurt her wonderful companions. And if it meant sacrificing her chance to change back, then so be it! She'd kinda got used to being tiny, anyway.

STEP TWO. Using all her might, Betty glared at the thorny wand. Then, in the firmest voice known to mankind, she said, **'BOG OFF!'**

Ooooh-eeeee, that wand began to sizzle! The witch yelped and dropped it.

'What did you do?!' she shouted.

The weeds fizzed and hissed and muttered 'Crikey' under their breath. Then, in a puff of smoke, they disintegrated into a pile of crusty soot.

As the Toad Witch looked down at the remains of her wand, the citizens of Wobbly Rock gave a massive cheer. King Nutmeg blew a jolly raspberry. Pam jumped on Pamm's back and started a chant of BOOGLE-OOGLE-BLIM-BLAM. And Johnny Logflume waved his flag as though he'd just invented the concept of happiness.

'LEAVE AND NEVER COME BACK!' said Betty, giving the witch a big shove in the leg for good measure.

Realising she was well and truly thrashed, the

Toad Witch crossed her arms. 'Not fair.'

Nim was furious and dropped Figg and Elle Emen-O'Pea to the ground. 'Come on, Mum, let's just go,' he muttered. 'You are SO embarrassing.'

The Toad Witch limped down the mountain after her son. 'Can I lean on you, Nim? I've got twigs in my feet.'

'Get OFF me. Ugh, I'm starving. And don't tell me we've got fish pie at home. I hate fish pie . . .'

As the sound of toady whinging faded into the distance, the Crossword Crew formed a friendship circle and sang *Ring a Ring o' Roses*.

'Oh, Great Guardian,' said Figg. 'You may be small, but you have brains, biceps and a can-do attitude. I never should have doubted you.'

Betty was pleased as poppadoms. 'And I couldn't have done it without my brilliant pals.'

eader, I want you to visualise what happened next . . . Imagine the citizens of Wobbly Rock, haunted by the horror of battle. Sad faces everywhere. The castle quiet and sombre, like a drizzly Monday morning. Now, I want you to imagine the exact opposite of that. Because everyone PARTIED THEIR FACES OFF!

After a traditional feast of chips and gravy, the fizzy pop began to flow! Betty sat with all her

brilliant pals. She even shared a fruit-corner yoghurt with Figg, who spent most of the evening telling Henry the paper clip all about his adventures.

When everyone was suitably merry, King Nutmeg raised his glass. 'TO THE CROSSWORD CREW!'

'THE FLOSS BIRD SHOE!' cried Lady Mayfly, after one too many cherryades.

'Your Majesty?' said a little voice from the floor.

The king looked down to see Elle Emen-O'Pea. 'Yes, small rodent?'

'Do you think we have time for a song?' asked the field mouse.

The room went quiet as the king thought very hard and did some complicated multiplication. 'Yes,' he finally said. 'I believe we do.'

The mouse smiled and held up her instrument. *Once Upon a Waffle* carried across the great hall like the hearty smell of musical stew. As she tooted with her little mousey heart and soul, Elle Emen-O'Pea felt as though the trumpet was the meaning of life.

By the time the song came to its breathtaking climax, King Nutmeg's ears had begun to weep with joy. 'Well, I'll be a donkey's dentist!' he said, wiping his ears with a tissue. 'That was glorious. Little mouse, would you consider being my First Royal

Trumpeter? You know – the person who goes $\mathbb{DO}$-$\mathbb{DO}$-$\mathbb{DO}$-$\mathbb{DO}$ as I walk in?'

Elle Emen-O'Pea felt her heart doing jazz hands. DREAM COME TRUE!

Everybody gave another big cheer, Simon Anderson clapped his hooves, and Johnny Logflume said, 'This is the best darn day of my life!'

Before the night was through, the Crossword Crew were awarded gold medals for bravery. Then the Royal Chefs were awarded bold medals for gravy. Everything was wonderful.

'Hey, Crossword Crew,' said Pamm, tipping her bready crown at Betty, Figg, Elle Emen-O'Pea and Rupert Sometimes. 'Do you ALL want to come to ours for a sleepover tonight? We can play *pin the wig on the weasel*.'

Betty grinned. 'We'd love to. Unless, of course, something urgent and terrifying happens. Then we'd have to ride out and save the day as usual. But that's not likely anytime soon, is it? Haha!'

'Hahaha!' said the whole gang, as though they'd practised it at least thirty-seven times. 'No way.'

Suddenly, an enchanted boiled egg burst through the door.

Betty gasped. 'Has something urgent and terrifying happened?'

'Oh, sorry,' said the enchanted boiled egg. 'Wrong room. Carry on as you were.'

So, lovely reader, we have come to the end of this tale. I'm going to miss you all so much. I hate goodbyes. Maybe, if you're all good - and I can find another pen that works - I could tell you more tales of our Betty one day.

But, for now, you'll be glad to know that the Crossword Crew did play *pin the wig on the weasel* that night. And thereafter, they made an effort to spend every bin day together, doing crosswords, eating custard creams and having a right old laugh.

Although our mighty hero, Betty Steady, was still a tiny little thing, she was as happy as a hair bobble because she had a load of courage in her heart. And - most importantly - she had her special chums to help her LICK THE TOENAILS OF ADVENTURE!

THE END

figg's Bumbags

Cut them out and stick them on Figg!

Acknowledgements

First and foremost, I'd like to thank the dedicated researchers at the Library of Wobbly Rock for helping me pore over thousands of historical papers to ensure I got the details just right. (Hang on. I just remembered; I made it all up as I went along.)

Anyway, I'd like to thank 'Ideas Man' (my husband, Alex). You have supported and encouraged me every step of the way. Thank you for being the best sounding board. Pam and Pamm are forever grateful.

Mum. Thank you for being my first reader and greatest cheerleader. I don't know what I'd do without you. Dad. Thank you for filling our childhood with stories, stupid jokes and endless laughter. Carly. Thanks for being the most supportive and wonderful sister. We both know the Pickling Peril paved the way to success.

Thank you to all my brilliant friends, old and new, for shaping my sense of humour and giving me the confidence to put my writing out there. Shout out to my school pals for originating the eggy, figgy comedy style. Thank you to Cheryl for being my bestie, wifey and enthusiastic supporter. Thanks Jo A for our amazing writing sessions. You always made me feel so good about my work.

To my incredible agent, Kate. Thank you for giving a mad idea a chance. Your input has been invaluable and let's not forget, you named our proud heroine!

Lucy, thank you for being a Simon Anderson superfan and the perfect editor for Betty. You had such a great vision for the book and made it a trillion times better. I am so grateful to everyone at Farshore for all their hard work, including Ryan for his fab design work and Maddy, Samara and the publicity and marketing team.

Sarah, thank you for your incomparable illustrations. Even now, I weep with laughter at some of the little details. You have brought the book to life in ways that I never could have imagined.

Finally, I'd like to thank my children, Miles and Cassie. These books were written as I held you in my arms, and my love for you is on every page.

Nicky

More Crossword Crew
shenanigans coming soon!

BETTY STEADY

AND THE QUEEN'S ORB

GOLLY GHERKINS!

Nicky Smith-Dale

Nicky spent her childhood in daydreams, floating through life in a haze of stories and silliness. When she grew up (and had to impersonate a sensible adult) she tried a few uninspiring career options before discovering that teaching was a lot of fun. Then she decided to write a silly story about evil toads and enchanted boiled eggs and a hero called Betty Steady. It was weird but it worked I guess?

Sarah Horne

Sarah Horne learned to draw while trying to explain her reasoning for an elaborate haircut at the age of nine. She has illustrated over 100 books and started her career illustrating for newspapers. When not at her desk, Sarah loves running, painting, photography, cooking, film and a good stomp up a hill. She can mostly be found giggling under some paper in her London studio.